U0003634

英譯／泰戈爾 Tagore

中譯／萬源一

卡比爾
之歌

Kabir

Songs of Kabir

譯 序

　　卡比爾（Kabīr, 1398-1518），是印度的一個織布
工、詩人、神祕主義者、宗教改革家、聖人和上師。他
活了一百二十歲。

　　卡比爾所處的時代是一個社會動盪的時代，有關他
生平的記載很少，但許多有關他的傳說卻流傳至今。

　　卡比爾出生在印度東北部的貝拿勒斯（今瓦拉納
西），據說是一名婆羅門寡婦的兒子，出生後即被遺棄。
他被一個屬於久拉哈種姓的穆斯林家庭發現並收養。久
哈拉在波斯語中是織布工的意思，這是一個社會地位很
低下的種姓。他從未上過學，幾乎一字不識。

　　卡比爾長大以後，師從當時著名的婆羅門開悟者拉
瑪南達（Swami Rāmānanda）。拜師經過很具有傳奇
色彩：年輕的卡比爾來到恆河邊，在那裡等候拉瑪南達，
當拉瑪南達從恆河沐浴返回時，卡比爾突然上前抱住他
的腳。在恆河中沐浴是婆羅門神聖的宗教儀式，如果一
個婆羅門在剛沐浴之後被誰抱住了腳，他一定會勃然大
怒，但拉瑪南達是一個聖者，他問道：「我的孩子，你

想要做什麼?」卡比爾說:「先生,請收我為徒,我想悟道。」拉瑪南達當即答應了。但他的弟子們卻反對道:「先生,他是一個穆斯林、一個孤兒,你怎能收他為徒?他不會尊奉印度教的。」拉瑪南達看了一眼卡比爾,他看到了一個尋道者。他回答道:「你們並不瞭解他。我瞭解他。」於是卡比爾成了拉瑪南達的弟子。

卡比爾跟隨拉瑪南達許多年,他跟隨他的老師參加各種神學或哲學辯論,爭論的對象都是當時著名的毛拉(伊斯蘭教士)和婆羅門,他因此瞭解了印度教和蘇菲神祕主義思想。

在他悟道以後,他依然過著世俗的生活,依然靠織布維生。傳說他與一個名叫羅伊的女子結婚,生了兩個兒子。在他織布的時候,把布拿到市場上去賣的時候,他就在心中編織他的詩歌,然後把它們唱出來。人們圍在他的四周,聆聽他歌唱、講道。

卡比爾的追隨者日益增多,逐漸形成了龐大的卡比爾教派,也稱作聖道或聖人之路(Sant Mat)教派。

傳說卡比爾告別人世時,他還給世人留下了最後的啟示。在印度,人們相信,如果一個人死在聖城貝拿勒斯,他的靈魂就一定能獲得拯救,從此逃脫生死輪迴,許多印度人為此在臨死前來到這裡。卡比爾一生都居住在貝拿勒斯，但當死亡臨近時，他卻前往一個被人認為是貧瘠而晦氣的名叫馬格哈的地方。他對弟子們說：「如果心中有神，馬格哈和貝拿勒斯又有什麼區別？」

在他去世之後，他的印度教徒和穆斯林教徒為他的葬禮而爭執不休。印度教徒要將上師火化，而穆斯林學生則要將他土葬。但當他們揭開覆蓋卡比爾的屍布時，他們發現，屍布下只剩下一堆花束。穆斯林的追隨者們將一半花葬在墓中，而印度教徒則將另一半花束火化。

卡比爾首先是一個詩人，而非哲學家、理論家或神學家。我們正是通過他的詩篇而認識了一個偉大詩人的靈魂；反之，如果他的詩歌沒有道出更為深刻的智慧和真理，它們也不會流傳至今。

儘管卡比爾一生中一直在批評印度的各個宗教派別，抨擊當時宗教的陳腐教條和儀式，反對修行者禁欲苦修，但他依然受到各個教派的尊敬和推崇，原因很簡單，卡比爾道出了真理。

卡比爾是一個目不識丁的織布工，但這並沒有妨礙他成為一個悟道者，反而在某種程度上成就了一個宗教融合者和創新者。他沒有受經文教條的約束，而是努力去融合印度教和伊斯蘭教的觀念。他從印度教中吸收了輪迴和業報觀念，從伊斯蘭教中汲取了一神論、以及反對種姓制度和偶像崇拜等觀念。他致力於宣導一種新的宗教——真正的愛的宗教、心的宗教。他宣稱：「沒有愛的宗教就是異端。」

卡比爾反覆指出，不論是印度教徒還是穆斯林，他們都是在崇拜同一個神，只是神的名稱各不相同而已。在卡比爾看來，神無需遠求，因為祂無處不在，只等你去發現。

他要求人們放棄外在的儀式和苦行，去尋找更為內在的和靈性的東西。他向人們展現了通往與神合一的內心之路：在心中找到神，在愛中與神合一。卡比爾教導人們要認識自我或靈魂——它正是神在我們每一個人內心的展現。這樣的認知會引向開悟，並從幻相中解脫。

卡比爾的宗教思想對印度宗教產生了極其深刻的影響。錫克教的創教者那納克（Nanak, 1496-1539）繼承了卡比爾的宗教主張，創立了融合印度教對神的奉愛以及伊斯蘭教上帝無形論於一身的錫克教。

卡比爾並沒有因為獲得對神的神祕體悟而成為職業的神祕主義者，或為了修道而逃避世俗生活，而是將高度的靈性融入了普通的生活中。他既是詩人、音樂家，同時也是一個普通的織布工。他在日常生活中興高采烈地唱出了他的神聖的愛的歌曲。他堅持樸素簡單的生活，讚美家庭和日常生活的價值，因為它們為愛和解脫提供了機會。

卡比爾的修行之道就是專注音流瑜伽（Surat Sabda Yoga），心中懷著愛和奉獻，反覆念誦神的名字，以達成自我消解、與神融為一體。這是一條抵達一切生命和光的最初源頭的捷徑，其祕密在於，那個「無以名之者」在成為有名時，就以「夏白德」（Sabda）、「納姆」（Naam）、或者音流（WORD）示現。正是這個靈性之流創造了靈魂、創造了萬物，其根本屬性就是悅耳的音調和燦爛的光明。

卡比爾共有兩千多首詩歌和一千五百首對句（couplets）傳世。錫克教的聖經《聖典》中就收錄了五百首卡比爾的詩歌。在印度，卡比爾也許是一個被人引用最多的作家，他被尊崇為北印度語的詩歌之父。

在卡比爾所處的時代,經書都是用梵文書寫的,除了少數祭司和學者之外,大多數人都無法理解。卡比爾的詩歌以通俗的北印度語寫成,詩歌的對象是普通大眾。他以當時的口語將他所提倡的教義傳達出來,因此,他的詩歌大受歡迎,被人們廣為傳唱,以至世代相傳,流傳至今。

卡比爾的詩歌通常通俗易懂、簡明扼要、充滿活力。他善於在詩歌中運用日常生活中大家所熟知的事物來象徵和比喻深奧的神和靈魂的觀念。他從不引經據典,而是道出他的所見和體悟。

卡比爾詩歌中一個最大的主題就是試圖道出一個神祕主義者的「不可道之道」。卡比爾努力試圖向人們指出神的所在,以及通往神的道路。在卡比爾的詩歌中,宇宙就是至高者梵天所創造的一個永恆的愛和喜悅的遊戲。人們可以通過聆聽內心,在冥想中體驗到至福、光明和神的音樂,進入靈魂與神在永恆的愛的海洋中合一的境界。

這個譯本是印度詩哲泰戈爾由孟加拉語英譯而成。泰戈爾本人的宗教、哲學思想和詩歌創作就深受卡比爾的影響。要譯介這位偉大的古代印度詩人,除了泰戈爾之外，恐怕沒有更合適的人選了。可以說，這個譯本基本展現了卡比爾的詩歌成就，也為人們瞭解卡比爾的宗教思想和神祕經驗提供了一個很好的機會。

萬源一

序 言

一

　　卡比爾是印度神祕主義傳統中的一位傳奇人物，他
的詩集是首次（一九一五年）呈現在英語讀者面前。卡
比爾出生於貝拿勒斯，父母是穆斯林信徒，大約一四四
〇年，年輕的卡比爾成了當時著名的印度教苦行僧拉瑪
南達（Swami Rāmānanda）的弟子。拉瑪南達在印度
北部掀起了宗教復興運動。十二世紀婆羅門教的偉大改
革家羅摩奴闍（Rāmānuja）則早已在南方興起宗教復
興。這次復興一方面反對正統宗教日益嚴重的形式主義；
一方面強調心靈渴求，而非極端一元論吠檀多哲學所強
調的知性主義。拉瑪南達的學說認為，個人對毗濕奴的
虔誠奉獻，是神性本質在個人層面的顯現，即神祕的「愛
的宗教」以一定程度的靈性文化顯現在各處，信條和哲
學都無力扼殺它。

　　雖然這種奉獻是印度教與生俱來的，在《薄伽梵歌》
許多段落中多有表述，但中世紀宗教復興的一大特點，
就是宗教諸說的混合。據說拉瑪南達已將這一精神傳授

給了卡比爾。拉瑪南達似乎具有廣泛的宗教文化背景，充滿了傳教熱情。在他所生活的時代，偉大的波斯神祕主義者阿塔爾（Attār）、薩迪（Sādī）、賈拉魯丁‧魯米（Jalālu'ddīn Rūmī）和哈菲茲（Hāfiz）的熱情洋溢的詩歌和深刻的哲學思想對印度的宗教思想產生了巨大的影響，拉瑪南達夢想調和這種強烈的伊斯蘭神祕主義和婆羅門教的傳統神學。有些觀點認為，這些偉大的宗教領袖也受到了基督教思想和生活的影響，但權威學者對此觀點的看法有分歧，在此不贅述。但我們可以斷言，有兩到三股互不相容的靈性文化潮流在他們的教義中發生了劇烈的碰撞，正如猶太教思想和希臘思想在早期基督教教派中發生碰撞一樣。而卡比爾的天賦有一個顯著特點：他能夠在他的詩歌中將它們融合在一起。

卡比爾是一個偉大的宗教改革者，也是一個教派的創始人，這個教派至今還擁有近百萬北方印度教徒，他還是一個神祕主義詩人。和許多究竟實相的揭示者一樣，他痛恨宗教排外主義，他致力於讓人們重獲神子的自由，但尊崇他的追隨者們又在新的地方重新設置了他所努力要拆除的障礙。慶幸的是，作為他對究竟實相的洞見和他對愛的自然流露的表達，他美妙的詩歌流傳了下來。

正是靠這些詩歌，而不是他的教義和教導，他發出了對心靈的不朽呼喚。在這些詩歌中，他運用不加分別地取自印度教和伊斯蘭教中通俗易懂的比喻和宗教象徵，演繹了一系列的神祕情感：從對無限的超凡脫俗的熱情，到對神性的極其親密和個人化的認知。你無法判定，詩歌作者到底是婆羅門還是蘇菲，是吠檀多學家還是毗濕奴信徒。正如卡比爾自己所言，他是「安拉和拉姆的孩子」。他了悟和崇拜的至高無上的靈性是超越性的，他試圖讓他人的靈魂也獲得祂充滿喜悅的友誼，這至高的靈性涵蓋了全部的形而上學範疇、所有對信念的定義；而每一種描述都對那無限、單一的整體做出了貢獻，祂以不同的尺度向所有忠實信徒展現祂自己。

卡比爾的生平流傳著各種互相矛盾的傳說，沒有任何一個故事能得到驗證。其中有些故事來自印度教徒，另一些來自穆斯林信徒，有人稱他為蘇菲，也有人稱他為婆羅門。但是，從他的名字可以推斷他的祖先屬於穆斯林。最合理的推測是，他是貝拿勒斯一個穆斯林織布工所生或收養的孩子，而貝拿勒斯是他生活的主要城市。

在十五世紀的貝拿勒斯，印度一神教的融合趨勢得到了充分發展。蘇菲和婆羅門似乎引發了爭端：這兩個宗教門派中極具靈性的教徒經常辯論拉瑪南達的教義，當時，拉瑪南達已經聲名顯赫。年輕的卡比爾生來充滿宗教激情，他把拉瑪南達視為自己生命中的導師，但他知道，一位印度古魯（Guru，上師之意）接受穆斯林作為自己門徒的機會微乎其微。因此，他躲在拉瑪南達經常沐浴的恆河邊的台階旁。結果，當拉瑪南達走進恆河時，意外地踩在了他身上。拉瑪南達驚叫道：「拉姆！拉姆！」——他所崇拜的神的化身的名字。卡比爾於是宣稱，他已從拉瑪南達口中聽到了收他為徒的禱文。拉瑪南達的門徒被他這種舉動給惹惱了，他們都反對古魯收卡比爾為徒。而卡比爾用行動體現了拉瑪南達所宣揚的宗教融合思想，拉瑪南達於是收他為徒。儘管根據伊斯蘭教傳說，卡比爾後來的老師是著名的蘇菲聖人詹西的塔基（Takkī of Jhansī），但這位印度教聖人才是卡比爾在自己詩歌中所承認和感激的唯一老師。

我們所知的為數不多的卡比爾生平與許多現代東方神祕主義觀念相矛盾。在他的門徒階段，我們對他的靈性天賦如何得到培養一無所知。他似乎跟隨拉瑪南達很多年，參與他古魯與當時所有著名的毛拉和婆羅門的神學和哲學辯論。我們由此可推測，他瞭解印度教和蘇菲哲學。他不一定接受過傳統印度教或蘇菲思想的教育，但無論如何他顯然從沒有過禁欲苦行或遁世隱修的生活。一方面，他過著奉愛的內心生活，這一點表現在音樂和文字上，他是個音樂家，也是個詩人；另一方面，作為織布工，他過著勤勞的普通生活。所有的傳說在這一點上都是一致的：卡比爾是個織布工，樸實無華，目不識丁，以織布維生。就像帳篷匠保羅（Paul）、皮革匠波姆（Jakob Böhme）、修補匠班揚（John Bunyan）、織帶工特斯坦根（Gerhard Tersteegen），卡比爾知道如何把修行和手藝結合起來。他的工作幫助而非妨礙了他所熱衷的內心冥想。他痛恨單純的禁慾苦修，他並不是個苦行者，而是一個丈夫和父親，他的修行就是過普通的日常生活，他吟唱歌頌聖愛的詩歌。他的作品也印證了他過著平凡的生活，他反覆頌揚家庭日常生活的價值，以及它所帶來的愛與超脫的機會，同時他蔑視瑜伽行者的職業修行，他們「蓄著亂蓬蓬的鬍子，看上去像一頭山羊」，他蔑視所有認為應該逃離世界的人，因為這裡充滿了愛、喜悅和美，因為這裡正是尋求究竟實相的最佳劇場，而至高神性已「將祂愛的形式遍滿世界」（參見第 21、40、43、66、76 首）。

在當時，並不需要太多的苦行經驗，就能認識到這種態度的勇氣和獨創性。無論是印度教還是伊斯蘭教，從正統觀點來看，卡比爾顯然是個異教徒。他坦率地表明，他不喜歡所有制度化的宗教、所有表面化的儀式、所有外在的遵從——就像極端而嚴格的貴格教派那樣。在教會看來，他是一個危險人物。他反覆稱頌與神聖實相「單純的合一」，而這正是每一個靈魂的職責和喜樂，這樣的結合既不依賴於儀式，也不依賴於身體的禁慾。他所宣稱的神「既不在天房，也不在伽拉薩山」。那些尋求祂的人不需要長途跋涉，因為祂等著你在任何地方找到祂，「洗衣婦和木匠」要比自以為是的聖人更容易接近祂（參見第 1、2、41 首）。因此，這個目光極其尖銳的詩人譴責整個虔誠的印度教和穆斯林宗教組織——寺廟和清真寺、偶像和聖水、經文和祭司——這些都只是實相的替代品；沒有生命的東西阻隔在靈魂和靈魂之愛之間（參見第 42、65、67 首）——

　　　偶像都沒有生命，它們一言不發；

　　　我知道，因為我曾向它們哭喊過。

　　　《往世書》和《古蘭經》只是文字；

我已揭開布幕，我已看見。

　　這種事是任何有組織的教派所不能容忍的。卡比爾把他的主要據點設在貝拿勒斯——祭司勢力範圍的中心，所以他受到相當程度的迫害也就不足為奇了。有一個很著名的傳說，婆羅門派了美麗的名妓去引誘他，試圖敗壞他的名聲，結果名妓卻皈依了卡比爾，就像抹大拉的瑪利亞一樣，她突然被更高尚的愛所感化。這個故事表明了教會權力對他的恐懼和不滿。有一次，在施行了一個所謂的療癒奇蹟之後，卡比爾被控聲稱擁有神力，於是他被帶到了西甘達爾·洛迪（Sikandar Lodi）皇帝那裡。但是，相當開明的皇帝容忍了屬於他自己信仰的聖人的怪癖。穆斯林出身的卡比爾不屬於婆羅門權威，而且嚴格來說屬於蘇菲，而蘇菲被允許擁有極大的神學自由。因此，出於治安考慮，卡比爾被驅逐出貝拿勒斯，但他保住了性命。這似乎發生在一四九五年，當時他已經快六十歲了。這是他職業生涯中最後一個我們能夠確定的事件。此後，他似乎搬到了印度北部的不同城市，這裡成了一群門徒的中心。他作為愛的使徒和詩人的生活在流亡中繼續，正如他在一首詩中所說的那樣，這「從時間之始」就註定了。一五一八年，一個疾病纏身、雙手無力，無法再創作自己喜愛音樂的老人，死於戈勒克布林（Gorakhpur）附近的馬格哈（Maghar）。

關於他的葬禮，流傳著一個美麗的傳說。在他去世後，他的穆斯林門徒和印度教門徒就如何舉行他的葬禮發生了爭執。穆斯林信徒想要舉行火葬，印度教門徒希望土葬。正當他們爭論不休時，卡比爾突然在他們面前現身，他讓他們揭開屍布，看看下面躺著的是什麼。他們在原來放屍體的地方發現了一堆鮮花。於是，穆斯林信徒把其中的一半埋在了馬格哈，印度教門徒把另一半帶到聖城貝拿勒斯焚燒。卡比爾讓兩個偉大宗教中最美麗的教義變得芳香四溢，對於他的一生來說，這是一個完美的結局。

二

神祕主義詩歌可以被定義為：一方面，是對究竟實相的洞見的一種個人化的反應；另一方面，是作為一種預言的形式。因為神祕意識的特殊作用就是在兩個層次之間進行調諧，靠著對神的滿懷愛的崇拜一路追尋，回歸之後則把永恆的祕密告訴他人，因此，這種意識的藝術化的自我表達也具有雙重性。它們是愛情詩，但常常是蘊含傳教意味的愛情詩。

卡比爾的詩歌屬於這樣一種類型：它們同時是狂喜和慈愛的產物。它們由通俗的印地文而非用深奧的文學語言寫成，就像雅各內‧達‧托迪（Jacopone da Todì, 十三世紀義大利天主教詩人）和理查‧羅爾（Richard Rolle, 十四世紀英國神祕主義詩人）的白話詩，它們所針對的讀者是普通人，而非職業宗教階層。人們必定會被不斷運用來自普通生活、普遍經驗的意象所打動。通過簡單的比喻，通過不斷呼籲所有人都理解的需求、激情和關係——新郎和新娘、古魯和門徒、朝聖者、農夫、候鳥，他使人理解他對靈魂與至高神性交流的強烈信念。在他的宇宙中，沒有「自然」與「超自然」世界之間的隔閡，一切都是神的創造性遊戲的一部分，因此，即使在最微不足道的細節中，也能夠顯現這位遊戲者的心靈。

作為表現究竟實相的一種手段，這種心甘情願接受現實生活的傳統，是偉大的神祕主義者的共同特徵。對他們來說，當他們終於達成開悟，宇宙的各個面向都能道出神性臨在的聖潔聲明。他們對日常生活和物質象徵的無所畏懼的運用——往往令人震驚，甚至怪異而叛逆——與他們的精神生活的成就成正比。偉大的蘇菲們的作品，以及在雅各內·達·托迪、呂斯布魯克（Jan van Ruysbroeck）、波姆（Jakob Böhme）等基督徒的作品中大量存在這一規律的例證。因此，我們無需驚訝於在卡比爾詩歌中發現他竭力試圖表達他的狂喜、並想要與他人分享——具體和形而上學語言的不斷並列，在強烈的擬人化、微妙的哲學方式之間迅速轉換以領會人類與神性的交流。對這種轉換的需要、以及自然而然的運用，都植根於他對神的本質的觀念或洞見。除非我們努力了解這一點，否則我們不會深入理解他的詩歌。

卡比爾屬於為數不多的神祕主義開悟者——其中聖奧古斯丁（St. Augustine, 354-430，北非希波的基督教神學家）、呂斯布魯克和蘇菲派詩人賈拉魯丁·魯米也許是主要人物——他們已經成為所謂的看見神的人。他們解決了個人與非個人、超越與內在、神性本質的動與靜、哲學的絕對性和奉愛宗教的「真正的朋友」之間的無窮無盡的對立。他們做到了，不是通過一個接一個地談論這些明顯不相容的觀念，而是像呂斯布魯克所說的那樣：「在統一中融合」，通過提升到一個他們所具有的靈性直覺的高度，並被視為是一個完美整體的完全對立。這就需要——卡比爾和呂斯布魯克都明確承認——一個三層秩序的宇宙：成為、存在和「超存在」神性（參見第7、49首）。在這裡，神性被認為不是最終極的抽象，而是一個實存。祂啟發、支撐、並確實居住於相續、受限、有限的成為的世界和非受限、非相續、無限的存在的世界，卻又完全超越兩者。祂是一個無所不在的實存，祂是「全能者」，在祂內在，「星星就像露珠」。在祂的個人面向，祂是「心愛的托缽僧」，教導和陪伴每一個靈魂。祂被視為與生俱來的靈性，祂是「心靈中的心靈」。但是，所有這些都只是祂的本性的部分面向，它們是互補的：正如基督教教義中的聖三（與這一神學圖解驚人相似）代表了神聖一體的不同和互補的經驗。正如呂斯布魯克所說的一個實相層面，在那裡，「我們不能再說聖父、聖子和聖靈，而只能說唯一的存在，聖三的本質。」所以，卡比爾說：「祂超越了有限和無限，祂是純粹的存在。」（參見第7首）

　　相對於「有限與無限只有一字之差」，梵天是難以言喻的事實，同時又是絕對論哲學中的至高神性，也是個體靈魂的摯愛——正如一個基督教神祕主義者所言：

「對所有人來說都是共同的，對每個人來說又是特別的。」卡比爾能用這兩種方式來描述究竟實相，證明了他靈性經驗的豐富性和平衡性；它不是宇宙性的或擬人化的象徵所能單獨表達的。比絕對更絕對，比人類心靈更個人化，因此梵天既囊括、又超越了所有哲學概念、所有充滿熱情的內在直覺。祂是偉大的肯定、能量的源泉、生命和愛的源頭、願望的獨特滿足。祂的創造性詞彙是「唵」（Om），或者說，「永遠的是」。消極哲學剝離了神性本質的所有屬性，只通過祂不是什麼來定義祂是什麼，這把祂削減成了一種「虛空」，這對於詩人卡比爾來說是不可接受的。他說：梵天，「在抽象的觀念中，你永遠不會找到祂。」祂是遍滿世界的合一之愛，只有愛的眼睛才能領悟祂的完滿。那些了知祂的人從而將其分享出來，儘管他們可能永遠也無法說出那喜悅且妙不可言的宇宙之密。（參見第 7、26、76、90 首）

卡比爾可說是在神性本質的個人面向與宇宙面向之間達成了這種綜合，避開威脅神祕主義宗教的三大危險。

首先，他避免了過度的情感主義，一種排他的擬人化的奉獻傾向，這種奉獻是對神性人格的無限制的崇拜，尤其是對一種化身的崇拜；在印度可以看到極其誇張的對黑天神（Krishna）的崇拜，在歐洲則是對某些基督教聖人用情過度。

其次，他沒有受純粹一元論的靈魂消亡論的影響，如果按邏輯推論，那麼這一結論是不可避免的。換句話說，神與靈魂是同質的，而靈魂生命的目標就是被神性存在完全吸收。這也體現在吠陀哲學的「汝即彼」的觀念中。但卡比爾說，梵天和造物「相異，而又合一」；智者知道，靈性和物質世界「都是祂的腳凳」（參見第7、9首）。靈魂與祂的合一是愛的合一，是互為居所；所有神祕主義宗教所表達的實質上是二元論關係，而非一種人格沒有容身之地的自我消融。這一不變的區別——神性與靈魂之間神祕的分離中的合一，是所有神志清醒的神祕主義的必備學說。對此的肯定是羅摩奴闍所宣揚的毗濕奴教派改革的一個顯著特徵；這一原則已經由拉瑪南達傳給了卡比爾。

最後，在卡比爾的詩歌中，熱烈而又頻繁地表達了對神性——作為愛的最高對象、靈魂的同志、老師和新郎——的熱烈而直接的理解，這平衡和控制了他對究竟實相的洞見這一天生的形上學傾向，並防止它退化成知性形式的無知崇拜，而這成了吠陀學派的詛咒。他對知識份子和虔信派教徒幾乎沒有什麼好感（相較而言，尤其是第 59、67、75、90、91 首）。愛始終是他「絕對而唯一的主」、他所享受的更加豐富的生活的獨特源頭，以及將有限與無限世界相連的共同因素。一切都沉浸在愛中，這種愛是他幾乎用《約翰福音》的語言所描述的「神性的形式」。整個創造是永恆的愛者的遊戲，梵天的愛與喜悅的充滿活力、變化、成長的表達。由於這雙重激情主宰了人類的生活，超越了「歡樂與痛苦的迷霧」，所以，卡比爾發現它們管轄著神性的創造性活動。祂的表現就是愛，祂的活動就是喜悅。創造源自一種正向的快樂行為：永恆的是，永遠在神性本質深處言說（參見第 17、26、76、82 首）。根據宇宙是永遠在進行中的愛和遊戲——梵天的持續顯現——的觀念，他從印度教借用的許多觀念之一，經由他富於詩歌天賦的描繪，運動、節奏和永恆的變化形成了卡比爾對實相的洞見的不可分割的一部分。雖然永恆與絕對對於他的意識是永遠臨在的，但他對神性本質的觀念根本上是動態的。他經常用運動的象徵來把這一觀念傳達給我們：正如他不斷提及跳舞或宇宙的永恆鞦韆的意象。（參見第 17 首）

神祕主義文學的一個顯著特徵就是，偉大的冥想家們在努力向我們傳達他們與究竟實相交流的本質時，會不可避免地使用某種形式的感官意象：它們粗糙而不準確，他們明白，即便是最好的意象也是如此。我們通常的人類意識完全依靠感官，並本能地把直覺認知與它們相對照。對神祕主義者來說，在這種直覺中，所有感覺的朦朧渴望和不完整理解都得到了完美的實現。因此，他們反覆聲明，他們看到了沒有被創造出來的光，他們聽到了天上的旋律，他們嘗到了主的甜蜜，他們聞到一種不可言喻的香味，他們感受到了愛的觸摸。正如諾維奇的朱利安（Julian of Norwich）所言：「祂被真正看到和充分感覺到，祂在靈性上被聽到，而且祂被甜美地嗅到和吞咽。」在那些培養直覺領悟力的人們當中，感官和精神之間的這些相似之處可以以幻覺形式呈現在意識中：就像蘇索（Suso）所看到的光、羅爾（Rolle）所聽到的音樂、西恩納的聖凱薩琳（St. Catherine of Siena）小屋中充滿著的天堂的香水味、聖方濟和聖德蘭感覺到的身上的聖傷。這些是象徵主義的過度戲劇化，在這之下，神祕主義者本能地將他的靈性直覺呈現於表面意識。於是，在他感覺最能表達實相的特殊感官知覺中，他獨特的特質出現了。

現在，我們可以想像，神祕主義者對靈性秩序的反應是如此廣泛而各不相同，卡比爾輪流運用了所有的感官象徵。他告訴我們，他已經「不用眼睛看見」梵天的光輝，品嘗了神聖的甘露，感受到了與實相的欣喜若狂的接觸，聞到了天堂的花香。但他本質上是一個詩人和音樂家，節奏、和諧對他來說是美和真理的外衣。因此在他的詩歌中，他表現得像理查·羅爾一樣，他首先是一個神祕主義音樂家。他反覆說，創造充滿音樂，創造就是音樂。在宇宙的中心，「潔白的音樂如花綻放」：愛編織著旋律，而解脫敲擊著時間。它可以在家裡，也可以在天堂聽到，由普通人的耳朵和苦行僧訓練有素的感覺辨別出來。而且，每個人的身體都是一把七弦琴，梵天──「一切音樂之源」──在其上彈奏音樂。卡比爾到處都能聽到「不奏自響的無限的音樂」──天使演奏給聖方濟的那種天籟般的旋律，那充滿了羅爾靈魂的欣喜若狂的幽靈般的交響樂。（參見第 17、18、39、41、54、76、83、89、97 首）他採用並不斷提及印度教神廟中的一個形象──神聖的長笛演奏者黑天神。（參見第 50、53、68 首）他把天上的音樂在視覺上的呈現看作是宇宙在梵天面前所跳的神祕舞蹈。這既是一種崇拜的行為，也是普遍存在的神性其無限狂喜的一種表現。

　　然而，在這個廣泛而激昂的宇宙景象中，卡比爾從來不會失去與日常生活的聯繫，永遠不會忘記平常人的生活。他的腳已牢牢地站在大地上；他高尚而熱烈的領悟力始終由理性而充滿活力的智力活動、由真正的神祕主義者的天才所擁有的敏銳常識所操控。對簡單性和直接性的不懈堅持、對所有抽象和哲學的憎恨、（參見第26、32、76首）對外在宗教的嚴厲批判，這些都是他最為顯著的特徵。神性是神聖根源，而所有「物質的」和「靈性的」彰顯都發源於此；神性是人類唯一的需要──「當你來到樹根，幸福就會屬於你。」（參見第80首）因此，對於那些專注於「唯一需要的東西」的人來說，教派、信仰、儀式、哲學論斷、禁欲戒律，都是相對不重要的事情。它們僅僅代表了靈魂可以達成與梵天合一的不同角度。而靈魂的目標就是與梵天合一，只有在它們有助於靈魂達成合一的情況下才有用。卡比爾的折衷主義極其徹底，他似乎既是吠檀多學家，又是毗濕奴派信徒；既是泛神論者，又是超驗主義者；既是婆羅門，又是蘇菲。究竟實相操控著他的生活，它如此廣大，但又如此接近，為了說出不可言說的對實相的領悟，他抓住它並與它纏繞在一起，就像他在織布機上紡織不同的經線和緯線——從極端和充滿衝突的哲學和信仰中抽出的象徵和觀念。如果他想要描繪《奧義書》中所說的「超越這黑暗的太陽般的神性存在」的性格，那所有這些都是需要的，正如如果我們要表現白光簡單的豐富性，那麼光譜中的所有顏色就都需要一樣。因此，為了讓傳統的材料能為他所用，他遵循神祕主義者常用的一個方法：他們很少表現出對形式的原創性的特別偏愛；他們會把葡萄酒倒入幾乎所有可用的容器中，一般來說，好用就行，並提升到美和重要性的新層次——即當時的宗教或哲學形式。因此，我們發現卡比爾的一些最好的詩歌是以印度哲學和宗教的共同點作為它們的主題：神的遊戲、至福的海洋、靈魂之鳥、幻相、百瓣蓮花以及「無形之形」。許多主題也來自於蘇菲的意象和感覺；另一些則以印度生活中常見的環境和事件為材料：寺廟的鐘聲、燃燈儀式、婚姻、受難、朝聖、季節的特點等。他能感受所有這些的神祕面向——作為靈魂與梵天關係的聖禮。在其中，許多呈現為對大自然的一種特別美好而親密的感情。（參見第 15、23、67、87、97 首）

　　在這本詩歌集中可以找到許多例子，這些例子幾乎可以說明卡比爾思想的各個方面，以及神祕主義者情感的所有波動：狂喜、絕望、寧靜的幸福、對自我奉獻的渴望、光明顯現、親密之愛的片刻。可以看出，他對宇宙、創造的「喜悅的遊戲」（參見第 82 首）、在神性存在內在的「就像露珠的星星」的寬廣而深刻的洞見，（參見第 14、16、17、76 首）被他與神聖的朋友、摯愛、靈魂導師的親密交流的可愛而微妙的感覺所平衡。（參見第 10、11、23、35、51、85、86、88、92、93 首；尤其是美麗的第 34 首）因為這些對究竟實相的顯然自相矛盾的觀點在梵天之中得到了解決，因此，所有其他對立在祂內在也得以和解：束縛與自由，愛與超脫，快樂與痛苦。（參見第 17、25、40、79 首）與祂合一是對靈魂及其命運、它的需要唯一至關重要的事；（參見第 51、52、54、70、74、93、96 首）而這種合一、這種對神性的發現，是所有事情中最簡單、最自然的，只要我們能把握住它。（參見第 41、46、56、72、76、78、97 首）但是，合一是由愛而非知識或儀式帶來的；（參見第 38、54、55、59、91 首）而這樣的合一所賦予的領悟是不可言說的──就像呂斯布魯克所言：「既非此，也非彼。」（參見第 9、46、76 首）真正的崇拜和交流是在靈性和真理中，（參見第 40、41、56、63、65、70 首）因此，偶像崇拜是對神性摯愛的侮辱，（參見第 42、49 首）而離開了靈魂的純潔和慈善，教條和儀式是徒勞無益的。（參見第 54、65、66 首）因為所有事物，特別是人類的心靈，是神性所居住和擁有的地方，（參見第 26、56、76、89、97 首）最好在此時此地找到祂——在正常人的肉身生活中、在物質生活的「泥潭」中。（參見第 3、4、6、21、39、40、43、48、72 首）「我們不用跨上路就能抵達目的」（參見第 76 首）——不是遁世隱修，而是家庭才是人類修行的合適場所；而如果他無法在這裡找到神性，他走得更遠就更加沒有成功的希望。「家就是真實。」在這裡，有愛和解脫、束縛和自由、喜悅和痛苦輪流與靈魂相伴遊戲，而無限的不奏自響的音樂正是來自於它們的衝突之中。卡比爾說：「除了梵天，無人能將它彈奏。」

三

卡比爾的這本詩歌集主要是泰戈爾先生的譯作，他的神祕主義天賦使他——正如所有讀過這些詩歌的人都會明白——成了對卡比爾的洞見和思想的獨到解讀者。
這本書是基於印地語文本加上凱西提・默罕・森先生
（Kshiti Mohan Sen）的孟加拉語翻譯；他從許多來
源收集卡比爾的詩歌——有時是從書本和手稿，有時是
從苦行僧和吟遊詩人的口中——大量詩歌和頌詩都與卡
比爾的名字聯繫在一起，他從當前被歸在卡比爾名下的
許多偽託作品中仔細篩選出了真實可信的卡比爾詩歌，
正是他的這些艱苦勞作才使本詩集的出版變得可能。我
們還收到了由阿吉特・庫馬爾・查克拉瓦蒂先生（Ajit
Kumâr Chakravarty）從凱西提・默罕・森先生的譯本
中選譯的一一六首英文詩手稿，以及他寫的一篇有關卡
比爾的文章。我們從這些資料得到了很大的幫助。我們
已經從中選用了相當多的內容；而這篇文章所提到的幾
個事實已被納入到這篇序中。我們非常感謝阿吉特・庫
馬爾・查克拉瓦蒂先生以極其慷慨和無私的態度將他的
譯作交由我們處理。

英國基督教神祕學家 伊芙琳・恩德曉

（Evelyn Underhill, 1875-1941）

卡比爾之歌

I.13. mo ko kahāṉ dhūṉro bande*

O SERVANT, where dost thou seek Me?

Lo! I am beside thee.

I am neither in temple nor in mosque; I am
    neither in Kaaba nor in Kailash:

Neither am I in rites and ceremonies, nor in Yoga
    and renunciation.

If thou art a true seeker, thou shalt at once see
    Me: thou shalt meet Me in a moment of
    time.

Kabir says, "O Sadhu ! God is the breath of all
    breath."

❋ 英文詩序號及首行，出處為：Santiniketana; *Kabir* by Sri Kshi-timohan Sen, 4 parts, Brahmacharyas'rama, Bolpur, 1910-11，下同。

001

哦，僕人，你要在哪裡找尋我[1]？
瞧！我就在你身邊。
我既不在神廟裡，也不在清真寺；
我既不在天房[2]，也不在伽拉薩山[3]：
我不在禮拜和儀式中，
也不在瑜伽和苦行中。
如果你是真正的尋求者，
你會即刻看見我，
你會在一瞬間與我相遇。
卡比爾說：「哦，苦行僧，
神是所有呼吸的呼吸。」

I.16. Santan jāt na pūcho nirguṇiyāṉ

IT is needless to ask of a saint the caste to which
  he belongs;
For the priest, the warrior, the tradesman, and
  all the thirty-six castes, alike are seeking for
  God.
It is but folly to ask what the caste of a saint may
  be;
The barber has sought God, the washer-woman,
  and the carpenter——
Even Raidas was a seeker after God.
The Rishi Swapacha was a tanner by caste.
Hindus and Moslems alike have achieved that
  End, where remains no mark of distinction.

002

不要打聽一位聖人屬於哪個種姓；

因為祭司、武士、商人，以及所有三十六種姓，

都同樣在尋找神。

問一位聖人是什麼出生何其愚蠢；

剃頭匠、洗衣婦、木匠都尋找過神——

甚至拉維達斯[4]也追尋過神。

要說種姓，斯瓦帕泰仙人曾是一個皮革匠。

印度教徒、穆斯林同樣抵達了究竟之境，

那裡沒有種姓之分。

I.57. sādho bhāī, jīval hī karo āśā

O FRIEND! hope for Him whilst you live, know
  whilst you live; understand whilst you live: for in
  life deliverance abides.
If your bonds be not broken whilst living, what hope
  of deliverance in death?
It is but an empty dream, that the soul shall have
  union with Him because it has passed from the
  body.
If He is found now, He is found then,
If not, we do but go to dwell in the City of Death.
If you have union now, you shall have it hereafter.
Bathe in the truth, know the true Guru, have faith in
  the true Name!
Kabir says: "It is the Spirit of the quest which helps;
  I am the slave of this Spirit of the quest."

003

哦，朋友！在你有生之年，你要期盼祂，

在你有生之年，你要知曉祂；

在你有生之年，你要瞭解祂：

因為你可以在你活著時獲得解脫。

如果在你有生之年，你沒有掙脫束縛，

那你怎能寄望於死後得到解脫？

這只是癡人說夢——

認為死後靈魂會與神結合，因為它已離開肉身。

如果你此刻找得到祂，死後你也能。

否則，我們只能前往死亡之城。

如果你此刻就與祂合一，

從此你再也不會和祂分離。

在真理之中沐浴，結識真正的古魯，

信仰神的真名！

卡比爾說：「探求靈性才有所助益；

我是靈性探求的奴僕。」

I.58. bāgo nā jā re nā jā

Do not go to the garden of flowers!

O Friend! go not there;

In your body is the garden of flowers.

Take your seat on the thousand petals of the

   lotus, and there gaze on the Infinite Beauty.

004

不要前往花園！
哦，朋友！不要前往；
你的身體就是一座花園。
讓自己端坐於千瓣蓮花之上，
凝視無限之美。

I.63. avadhū, māyā tajī na jāy

TELL me, Brother, how can I renounce Maya?

When I gave up the tying of ribbons, still I tied
   my garment about me;

When I gave up tying my garment, still I covered
   my body in its folds.

So, when I give up passion, I see that anger
   remains;

And when I renounce anger, greed is with me
   still;

And when greed is vanquished, pride and
   vainglory remain;

When the mind is detached and casts Maya away,
   still it clings to the letter.

Kabir says, "Listen to me, dear Sadhu! the true
   path is rarely found."

005

告訴我，兄弟，

我如何能從幻相中解脫？

當我不再將衣帶打結，我還在裹緊我的衣袍；

當我不再裹緊我的衣袍，我還在用它遮體。

當我不再充滿熱情，我的憤怒並未離去；

當我擺脫了憤怒，貪婪依然伴我左右；

當貪婪消失，自負和傲慢還在；

當心智擺脫了幻相[5]，它還迷戀著文字。

卡比爾說：「請聽我說，

親愛的苦行僧，正道何其難覓！」

I.83. candā jhalkai yahi ghaṭ māhīṉ

THE moon shines in my body, but my blind eyes
    cannot see it:
The moon is within me, and so is the sun.
The unstruck drum of Eternity is sounded within me,
    but my deaf ears cannot hear it.

So long as man clamours for the I and the Mine, his
    works are as naught;
When all love of the I and the Mine is dead, then the
    work of the Lord is done.
For work has no other aim than the getting of knowledge:
When that comes, then work is put away.

The flower blooms for the fruit: when the fruit comes,
    the flower withers.
The musk is in the deer, but it seeks it not within itself:
    it wanders in quest of grass.

006

月亮照耀在我身上，但我眼盲看不見它：
月亮就在我內在，太陽也是一樣。
我內在的永恆之鼓不敲自響，
但我耳聾聽不到它。

只要人還在追求自我和名利，
他的工作就還沒有開始；
當對自我和名利的愛脫落殆盡，
真主的工作就已完成。
因為除了獲得真知，工作沒有其他目的：
當真知來臨，工作就告結束。

開花是為了結果：
當結出了果實，花兒就會凋零。
麝香就在麝鹿的身上，
但牠不在自己身上尋找，卻在草叢中徘徊。

I.85. sādho, Brahm alakh lākhāyā

WHEN He Himself reveals Himself, Brahma
  brings into manifestation That which can
  never be seen.
As the seed is in the plant, as the shade is in
  the tree, as the void is in the sky, as infinite
  forms are in the void——
So from beyond the Infinite, the Infinite comes;
  and from the Infinite the finite extends.

The creature is in Brahma, and Brahma is in
  the creature: they are ever distinct, yet ever
  united.
He Himself is the tree, the seed, and the germ.
He Himself is the flower, the fruit, and the shade.
He Himself is the sun, the light, and the lighted.
He Himself is Brahma, creature, and Maya.

007

當梵天[6]揭開祂自己，
祂就會帶入顯化。
正如種子在植物中，樹蔭在樹下，
虛空在空中，無限的形式在虛空之中——
因此，無限來自於無限之外；
而有限是由無限而來。

造物在梵天之中，
梵天在造物之內：
它們相異，而又合一。
祂自己就是樹、種子、幼芽。
祂自己就是花、果實、樹蔭。
祂自己就是太陽、陽光和被照耀者。
祂自己就是梵天、造物和幻相。

He Himself is the manifold form, the infinite
   space;
He is the breath, the word, and the meaning.
He Himself is the limit and the limitless: and
   beyond both the limited and the limitless is
   He, the Pure Being.
He is the Immanent Mind in Brahma and in the
   creature.

The Supreme Soul is seen within the soul,
The Point is seen within the Supreme Soul,
And within the Point, the reflection is seen again.
Kabir is blest because he has this supreme vision!

祂自己就是種種形式、無限的空間；

祂自己就是呼吸、音流[7]和意義。

祂自己就是有限和無限：

祂超越了有限和無限，

祂是純粹的存在。

祂是梵天和造物的內在心智。

在靈魂之內能看見至高靈魂，

在至高靈魂之內能看見靈點，

在靈點之內，重又能看見它的反映。

卡比爾是有福的，

因為他已看見至高之絕妙！

I.101. is ghaṭ antar bāg bagīce

WITHIN this earthern vessel are bowers and
   groves, and within it is the Creator:
Within this vessel are the seven oceans and the
   unnumbered stars.
The touchstone and the jewel-appraiser are
   within;
And within this vessel the Eternal soundeth, and
   the spring wells up.
Kabir says: "Listen to me, my friend! My beloved
   Lord is within."

008

在這大地之舟中，有涼亭和樹叢，

在它之內是造物主：

在這條船中，是七大海洋和無數星辰。

其中有試金石和鑒寶人；

在這條船中，永恆在發出聲響，泉水在噴湧。

卡比爾說：「我的朋友，請聽我說！

我摯愛的真主就在我心中。」

I.104. aisā lo nahīṉ taisā lo

O HOW may I ever express that secret word?

O how can I say He is not like this, and He is
like that?

If I say that He is within me, the universe is
ashamed;

If I say that He is without me, it is falsehood.

He makes the inner and the outer worlds to be
indivisibly one;

The conscious and the unconscious, both are His
footstools.

He is neither manifest nor hidden, He is neither
revealed nor unrevealed:

There are no words to tell that which He is.

009

哦，我如何才能道出這個神祕的字？
哦，我如何能說：
祂不像是這樣、祂像是那樣？
如果我說，祂在我之內，
就會讓宇宙蒙羞；
如果我說，祂在我身外，
這又是在說謊。
祂讓內在和外在世界成為不可分的一體；
意識和非意識，都是祂的腳凳。
祂既沒有顯現，也沒有隱藏，
祂既沒有揭開，也沒有掩蓋；
沒有文字可以說清祂是什麼。

I.121. tohi mori lagan lagāye re phakīr wā

To Thee Thou hast drawn my love, O Fakir!

I was sleeping in my own chamber, and Thou
didst awaken me; striking me with Thy
voice, O Fakir!

I was drowning in the deeps of the ocean of this
world, and Thou didst save me: upholding
me with Thine arm, O Fakir!

Only one word and no second——and Thou hast
made me tear off all my bonds, O Fakir!

Kabir says, "Thou hast united Thy heart to my
heart, O Fakir!"

010

哦，托缽僧，你已讓我愛上了你！
我本來在自己家裡睡覺，是你喚醒了我；
哦，托缽僧，是你的聲音把我喚醒！
我本來在人世的汪洋中溺水，是你救了我：
哦，托缽僧，是你伸手攙扶了我！
只有一個字，沒有第二個字——
哦，托缽僧，你已讓我掙脫所有束縛！
卡比爾說：「哦，托缽僧，
你已將你我的心相連！」

I.131. niś din khelat rahī sakhiyāṉ saṅg

I PLAYED day and night with my comrades, and
   now I am greatly afraid.
So high is my Lord's palace, my heart trembles
   to mount its stairs: yet I must not be shy, if I
   would enjoy His love.
My heart must cleave to my Lover; I must
   withdraw my veil, and meet Him with all
   my body:
Mine eyes must perform the ceremony of the
   lamps of love.
Kabir says: "Listen to me, friend: he understands
   who loves. If you feel not love's longing for
   your Beloved One, it is vain to adorn your
   body, vain to put unguent on your eyelids."

011

我和我的同道日夜遊玩，

如今，我陷入恐慌。

真主的殿堂高高在上，

在登天的階梯上，我的心在顫抖：

如果我能享有祂的愛，我又何需害羞。

我的心一定要緊緊纏住我的真愛；

當我遇見祂，我一定要

揭開我的面紗，整個身與祂相見：

我的雙眼一定要用愛之燈盞舉行慶典。

卡比爾說：「朋友，請聽我說，

只有戀人才會明白。

如果你感覺不到對摯愛的愛的渴望，

打扮你的身體也是徒勞，

用油膏塗抹你的眼瞼也是無益。」

II.24. haṃsā, kaho purātan bāt

TELL me, O Swan, your ancient tale.

From what land do you come, O Swan? to what
shore will you fly?

Where would you take your rest, O Swan, and
what do you seek?

Even this morning, O Swan, awake, arise, follow
me!

There is a land where no doubt nor sorrow have
rule: where the terror of Death is no more.

There the woods of spring are a-bloom, and
the fragrant scent "He is I" is borne on the
wind:

There the bee of the heart is deeply immersed,
and desires no other joy.

012

哦，天鵝[8]，向我講述你古老的故事。

哦，天鵝，你來自哪片土地？你要飛往哪個海濱？

哦，天鵝，你會在哪裡棲息？你在找尋什麼？

哦，天鵝，就在今晨醒來，起身，跟我來！

有一個地方，那裡沒有疑惑，也沒有悲傷：

那裡再也沒有恐怖的死亡。

在那裡，樹林開滿春花，

風中飄著「祂即我」的芬芳：

在那裡，心的蜜蜂深深陶醉，

不再希求別的快樂。

II.37. aṅgadhiyā devā

O LORD Increase, who will serve Thee?

Every votary offers his worship to the God
of his own creation: each day he receives
service——

None seek Him, the Perfect: Brahma, the
Indivisible Lord.

They believe in ten Avatars; but no Avatar can be
the Infinite Spirit, for he suffers the results
of his deeds.

The Supreme One must be other than this.

The Yogi, the Sanyasi, the Ascetics, are disputing
one with another.

Kabir says, "O brother! he who has seen that
radiance of love, he is saved."

013

哦，創造一切的真主，誰會服侍你？

每一個信神者都在崇拜他自己創造的神：

每一天他都得到服侍——

但沒有人尋求祂：完美的梵天，不可分的真主。

他們相信神的十個化身；

但沒有哪個化身會是無限靈性，

因為化身承受他自己的業報。

至高者絕非如此。

瑜伽行者、桑雅士[9]、苦行僧們在彼此爭論。

卡比爾說：「哦，我的兄弟！

誰看見愛的光芒，誰就得救。」

062
/
063

II.56. dariyā kī lahar dariyāo hai jī

THE river and its waves are one surf: where is
the difference between the river and its
waves?
When the wave rises, it is the water; and when it
falls, it is the same water again. Tell me, Sir,
where is the distinction?
Because it has been named as wave, shall it no
longer be considered as water?

Within the Supreme Brahma, the worlds are
being told like beads:
Look upon that rosary with the eyes of wisdom.

014

河流與它的波浪是同樣的海浪：

河流與波浪之間哪有不同？

當波浪升起，它是水；

當它落下，它還是同樣的水。

告訴我，區別在哪裡？

因為它被稱為波浪，它就不再被視為是水？

在至高梵天之中，世界被說成像是露水：

用智慧之眼，凝視玫瑰花園。

II.57. jāṇh khelat vasant ṛiturāj

WHERE Spring, the lord of the seasons, reigneth, there
the Unstruck Music sounds of itself,
There the streams of light flow in all directions;
Few are the men who can cross to that shore!
There, where millions of Krishnas stand with hands
folded,
Where millions of Vishnus bow their heads,
Where millions of Brahmās are reading the Vedas,
Where millions of Shivas are lost in contemplation,
Where millions of Indras dwell in the sky,
Where the demi-gods and the munis are unnumbered,
Where millions of Saraswatis, Goddess of Music, play
on the vina——
There is my Lord self-revealed: and the scent of sandal
and flowers dwells in those deeps.

015

春天這四季之王，它在哪裡統治，

無聲的音樂就在哪裡不奏自響，

哪裡就有光明四處流溢；

能抵達彼岸的人少之又少！

在那裡，千萬個黑天神[10]的信徒雙手合十站立，

在那裡，千萬個毗濕奴[11]的信徒在敬拜，

在那裡，千萬個婆羅門在誦讀《吠陀經》，

在那裡，千萬個濕婆神[12]的信徒沉醉在冥想中，

在那裡，千萬個因陀羅[13]居住在空中，

在那裡，半神和聖人數不勝數，

在那裡，千萬個妙音天女在彈奏七弦琴——

在那裡，我的真主揭開祂自己：

檀香瀰漫，花朵安憩於深處。

II.59. jānh cet acet khambh dōū

BETWEEN the poles of the conscious and the
   unconscious, there has the mind made a
   swing:
Thereon hang all beings and all worlds, and that
   swing never ceases its sway.
Millions of beings are there; the sun and the
   moon in their courses are there:
Millions of ages pass, and the swing goes on.
All swing! the sky and the earth and the air and
   the water; and the Lord Himself taking
   form:
And the sight of this has made Kabir a servant.

016

在意識和無意識的兩極之間，
心靈搭了一架鞦韆：
所有的生命、所有的世界
都懸在鞦韆上搖擺，從不停息。
上面搖擺著無數生命，
上面搖擺著日升月落：
億萬年過去，盪鞦韆依然持續。
一切都在擺盪！
天和地，水和空氣；而真主由此顯現：
這幅情景使卡比爾成為一名僕人。

II.61. grah candra tapan jot barat hai

THE light of the sun, the moon, and the stars shines
  bright:
The melody of love swells forth, and the rhythm of
  love's detachment beats the time.
Day and night, the chorus of music fills the heavens;
  and Kabir says,
"My Beloved One gleams like the lightning flash in the
  sky."

Do you know how the moments perform their
  adoration?
Waving its row of lamps, the universe sings in worship
  day and night,
There are the hidden banner and the secret canopy:
There the sound of the unseen bells is heard.
Kabir says: "There adoration never ceases; there the
  Lord of the Universe sitteth on His throne."

Songs of Kabir

017

日月星辰光明閃耀，

愛的旋律越來越響：

愛的超脫這一弦律戰勝了時間。

日日夜夜，美妙的音樂充滿天堂，

卡比爾說：「我的摯愛一閃即逝，

就像空中的閃電。」

你是否知道，每一個瞬間如何表達它們的愛慕？

宇宙日夜搖晃著它成排的燈盞，崇敬地歌唱，

那裡有隱蔽的旗幡和祕密的天篷：

那裡能聽到無形之鐘的鳴響。

卡比爾說：「在那裡，愛慕之情永不停息；

在那裡，宇宙的真主端坐在祂的高位上。」

The whole world does its works and commits its errors:
but few are the lovers who know the Beloved.

The devout seeker is he who mingles in his heart the
double currents of love and detachment, like the
mingling of the streams of Ganges and Jumna.

In his heart the sacred water flows day and night; and
thus the round of births and deaths is brought to
an end.

Behold what wonderful rest is in the Supreme Spirit!
and he enjoys it, who makes himself meet for it.

Held by the cords of love, the swing of the Ocean of
Joy sways to and fro; and a mighty sound breaks
forth in song.

See what a lotus blooms there without water! and Kabir
says,

"My heart's bee drinks its nectar."

整個世界都在運作，並且犯下錯誤：

但認識摯愛的戀人少之又少。

虔誠的尋求者讓愛和超脫在他心中匯流，

就像恆河與朱木納河 [14] 匯流。

在他心中，聖水日夜流淌；

於是，生死的輪迴就此停止。

看，在至高靈性中安息是何其美妙！

誰讓自己尋求它，誰就會安享其中。

繫住愛的繩索，歡樂海洋的鞦韆前後搖盪；

一聲巨響化作歌聲。

看，一朵無水之蓮綻放！卡比爾說：

「我心中的蜜蜂正在暢飲牠的花蜜。」

What a wonderful lotus it is, that blooms at the heart
of the spinning wheel of the universe! Only a few
pure souls know of its true delight.
Music is all around it, and there the heart partakes of
the joy of the Infinite Sea.
Kabir says: "Dive thou into that Ocean of sweetness:
thus let all errors of life and of death flee away."

Behold how the thirst of the five senses is quenched
there! and the three forms of misery are no more!
Kabir says: "It is the sport of the Unattainable One:
look within, and behold how the moonbeams of
that Hidden One shine in you."

There falls the rhythmic beat of life and death:
Rapture wells forth, and all space is radiant with light.
There the Unstruck Music is sounded; it is the music of
the love of the three worlds.
There millions of lamps of sun and of moon are
burning;

這朵蓮花何其美妙，盛開在宇宙轉輪的心中！

只有少數純潔的靈魂

才明白它真實的喜樂。

音樂將它圍繞，心兒分享無限海洋的喜悅。

卡比爾說：「你就躍入這甜蜜的海洋：

就此讓所有生死的過錯逃離。」

看，在那裡，感官的乾渴如何被澆熄！

不再有三大痛苦！

卡比爾說：「這是不可及者的運作：

向內看，注視著隱藏者的月光如何在你心照耀。」

在那裡，生與死敲打出旋律：

狂喜噴湧如泉，

空中充滿光明。

在那裡，音樂不奏自響；

這是三個世界的愛的樂曲。

在那裡，無數日月的燈盞在燃燒；

There the drum beats, and the lover swings in play.

There love-songs resound, and light rains in showers; and the worshipper is entranced in the taste of the heavenly nectar.

Look upon life and death; there is no separation between them,

The right hand and the left hand are one and the same.

Kabir says: "There the wise man is speechless; for this truth may never be found in Vedas or in books."

I have had my Seat on the Self-poised One,

I have drunk of the Cup of the Ineffable,

I have found the Key of the Mystery,

I have reached the Root of Union.

Travelling by no track, I have come to the Sorrowless Land: very easily has the mercy of the great Lord come upon me.

They have sung of Him as infinite and unattainable: but I in my meditations have seen Him without sight.

在那裡，鼓聲陣陣，戀人在嬉戲旋轉。

在那裡，愛的歌聲迴蕩，光芒如雨紛紛落下；

崇拜者因嘗到天堂的甘霖而狂喜。

看著生與死；

生與死之間沒有分隔，

正如左手與右手合一。

卡比爾說：「在那裡，智者無言；

因為這樣的真理無法從《吠陀經》

或其他書中找到。」

我已坐上自在者的座椅，

我已暢飲不可言說的杯盞，

我已找到神祕之鑰，

我已抵達合一之根。

走過烏有之徑，

我已來到無憂之地：

我輕易就得到了偉大真主的恩寵。

人們歌頌祂無限而高不可及：

但在冥想中，我已見到祂的無形之相。

That is indeed the sorrowless land, and none know the path that leads there:

Only he who is on that path has surely transcended all sorrow.

Wonderful is that land of rest, to which no merit can win;

It is the wise who has seen it, it is the wise who has sung of it.

This is the Ultimate Word: but can any express its marvellous savour? He who has savoured it once, he knows what joy it can give.

Kabir says: "Knowing it, the ignorant man becomes wise, and the wise man becomes speechless and silent,

The worshipper is utterly inebriated,

His wisdom and his detachment are made perfect;

He drinks from the cup of the inbreathings and the outbreathings of love."

那裡確實是無憂之地，

沒有人知道通往它的道路：

只有上路的求道者，才能超越所有痛苦。

那安息之地多麼美妙，

豐功偉績都無法贏得；

只有智者才目睹過它，

只有智者才歌頌過它。

它是究竟音流：

但有誰能道出它的絕妙？

只要嘗過一次，

他就明白它能帶來怎樣的喜悅。

卡比爾說：「明白了它，

無知者就會成為智者，

智者就會沉默不語，

崇拜者就會陶醉不已，

他的智慧和超脫就會變得完美；

他就會暢飲愛之呼吸的杯盞。」

There the whole sky is filled with sound, and there that
music is made without fingers and without strings;
There the game of pleasure and pain does not cease.
Kabir says: "If you merge your life in the Ocean of Life,
you will find your life in the Supreme Land of
Bliss."

What a frenzy of ecstasy there is in every hour! and
the worshipper is pressing out and drinking the ,
essence of the hours: he lives in the life of Brahma.
I speak truth, for I have accepted truth in life; I am now
attached to truth, I have swept all tinsel away.
Kabir says: "Thus is the worshipper set free from fear;
thus have all errors of life and of death left him."

There the sky is filled with music;
There it rains nectar:
There the harp-strings jingle, and there the drums beat.
What a secret splendour is there, in the mansion of the
sky!

在那裡，整個天空都充滿了樂音，

在那裡，音樂並不來自手指和琴弦；

在那裡，歡樂和痛苦的遊戲永不停息。

卡比爾說：「若你將你的生命融入生命的海洋，

你就會發現你身處極樂的天堂。」

在每一刻，都有強烈的狂喜！

崇拜者在榨取並啜飲光陰的精華：

他活在梵天的生命之中。

我已道出真理，因為我已接受了生命的真相；

如今我已與真理相連，

我已將所有華而不實的裝飾丟棄。

卡比爾說：「崇拜者就這樣擺脫恐懼，重獲自由；

生與死的所有過錯就這樣離他而去。」

在那裡，天空中充滿了音樂；

在那裡，甘霖如雨而下：

在那裡，琴聲悠揚，在那裡，鼓聲嘹亮。

在那裡，無比輝煌的祕密就在天庭裡！

There no mention is made of the rising and the setting
of the sun;
In the ocean of manifestation, which is the light of love,
day and night are felt to be one.
Joy for ever, no sorrow, no struggle!
There have I seen joy filled to the brim, perfection of
joy;
No place for error is there.
Kabir says: "There have I witnessed the sport of One
Bliss!"

I have known in my body the sport of the universe: I
have escaped from the error of this world.
The inward and the outward are become as one sky,
the Infinite and the finite are united: I am drunken
with the sight of this All!
This Light of Thine fulfils the universe: the lamp of love
that burns on the salver of knowledge.
Kabir says: "There error cannot enter, and the conflict
of life and death is felt no more."

無需說，那裡沒有日升日落；

在顯現的海洋，是愛的光芒，

日與夜合而為一。

只有永恆的喜悅，沒有悲傷，沒有掙扎！

在那裡，我看見完滿的喜悅溢出杯沿；

在那裡，過錯無處容身。

卡比爾說：「在那裡，

我已見證神的至福遊戲！」

我從我的身體知曉了宇宙的遊戲：

我已逃離這個世界的謬誤。

內在和外在成為一個天空，

無限和有限合而為一：

我因目睹這一切而陶醉！

你的光明充滿宇宙：

愛的燈火在知識的托盤上燃燒。

卡比爾說：「在那裡，錯誤無法進入，

不再有生與死的衝突。」

II.77. maddh ākāś āp jahāṉ baiṭhe

THE middle region of the sky, wherein the spirit
   dwelleth, is radiant with the music of light;
There, where the pure and white music blossoms,
   my Lord takes His delight.
In the wondrous effulgence of each hair of His
   body, the brightness of millions of suns and
   of moons is lost.
On that shore there is a city, where the rain of
   nectar pours and pours, and never ceases.
Kabir says: "Come, O Dharmadas! and see my
   great Lord's Durbar."

018

在蒼穹的中央，靈性的居所，

光明的音樂放射光芒；

在那裡，純粹潔白的音樂如花綻放，

真主喜悅開懷。

祂身體的每一根毛髮都散發出神奇的光芒，

令千萬個日月都變得黯淡無光。

在海邊有一座城市，甘霖傾盆而下，從不停歇。

卡比爾說：「哦，虔誠的人，來吧！

來與我偉大的真主相見。」

II. 20. paramātam guru nikat virājaiṇ

O MY heart! the Supreme Spirit, the great
Master, is near you: wake, oh wake!
Run to the feet of your Beloved: for your Lord
stands near to your head.
You have slept for unnumbered ages; this
morning will you not wake?

019

哦，我的心兒！
至高靈性，偉大的真主，
就在你身邊：
醒來，哦，醒來！
跑向你摯愛的腳前：
因為你的真主就站在你面前。
你已經沉睡了無數歲月；
你還不在今晨醒來？

II.22. man tu pār utar kāṇh jaiho

To what shore would you cross, O my heart? there is
  no traveller before you, there is no road:
Where is the movement, where is the rest, on that
  shore?
There is no water; no boat, no boatman, is there;
There is not so much as a rope to tow the boat, nor a
  man to draw it.
No earth, no sky, no time, no thing, is there: no shore,
  no ford!
There, there is neither body nor mind: and where is the
  place that shall still the thirst of the soul ? You shall
  find naught in that emptiness.
Be strong, and enter into your own body: for there your
  foothold is firm. Consider it well, O my heart! go
  not elsewhere.
Kabir says: "Put all imaginations away, and stand fast in
  that which you are."

020

哦，我的心兒，你將穿過哪個海岸？

在你之前沒有旅人，也沒有道路：

在海岸上你要在哪裡活動，又要在哪裡歇息？

那裡沒有水，沒有船，也沒有船夫；

那裡連拉船的繩子都沒有，更沒有拉船的人。

那裡沒有大地，沒有天空，沒有時間，沒有萬物：

那裡沒有海岸，沒有淺灘！

在那裡，沒有身體，沒有心靈：

哪裡是止息靈魂乾渴之地？

你無法在那片虛空中找到。

要堅強，進入你自己身體裡：

因為你能在那裡牢牢立足。

哦，我的心兒，好好想想！

不要去到別的地方。

卡比爾說：「丟開一切幻想，

牢牢站在你所在的地方。」

II.33. ghar ghar dīpak barai

LAMPS burn in every house, O blind one! and you cannot see them.

One day your eyes shall suddenly be opened, and you shall see: and the fetters of death will fall from you.

There is nothing to say or to hear, there is nothing to do: it is he who is living, yet dead, who shall never die again.

Because he lives in solitude, therefore the Yogi says that his home is far away.

Your Lord is near: yet you are climbing the palm-tree to seek Him.

The Brahman priest goes from house to house and initiates people into faith:

021

每一棟房屋都亮著燈盞，

哦，盲者！你卻看不見。

總有一天，你的眼睛會突然睜開，

你將會看見：

死亡的枷鎖將會從你身上脫落。

沒有什麼要說，沒有什麼要聽，也沒有什麼要做：

他是生者，但他已死，

他將永不再亡。

因為他活在孤獨之中，

所以瑜伽行者說，

他的家在遠方。

真主離你很近：

而你卻爬上棕櫚樹找祂。

婆羅門祭司走家串戶，奉勸人們信神：

Alas! the true fountain of life is beside you, and
you have set up a stone to worship.

Kabir says: "I may never express how sweet my
Lord is. Yoga and the telling of beads, virtue
and vice——these are naught to Him."

唉！真正的生命之泉就在你身邊，

你卻豎起石頭崇拜。

卡比爾說：「我恐怕永遠都無法表達出

真主是多麼可愛。

瑜伽和念珠、善和惡——

對於祂，這些都徒勞無益。」

II.38. sādho, so satgur mohi bhāwai

O BROTHER, my heart yearns for that true
Guru, who fills the cup of true love, and
drinks of it himself, and offers it then to me.

He removes the veil from the eyes, and gives the
true Vision of Brahma:

He reveals the worlds in Him, and makes me to
hear the Unstruck Music:

He shows joy and sorrow to be one;

He fills all utterance with love.

Kabir says: "Verily he has no fear, who has such a
Guru to lead him to the shelter of safety!"

022

哦，兄弟，我的心渴望真正的古魯，

他將真愛的杯盞斟滿，

將它品嘗，然後遞給我。

他揭開遮擋眼睛的面紗，

向你展現梵天的真容：

他顯現祂內在的世界，

讓我聆聽不奏自響的音樂：

他讓我看見，悲喜本是一體；

他的每一句話都滿含著愛。

卡比爾說：「誰能有這樣一位古魯，

指引他領受平安的庇護，

確實，他將不再有恐懼！」

II.40. tinwir sāñjh kā gahirā āwai

THE shadows of evening fall thick and deep, and
the darkness of love envelops the body and
the mind.

Open the window to the west, and be lost in the
sky of love;

Drink the sweet honey that steeps the petals of
the lotus of the heart.

Receive the waves in your body: what splendour
is in the region of the sea!

Hark! the sounds of conches and bells are rising.

Kabir says: "O brother, behold! the Lord is in this
vessel of my body."

023

夜幕深重，愛的黑暗將身心包圍。

打開西窗，沉湎於愛的蒼穹中；

暢飲浸漬心蓮的蜜露。

接納你內心的波濤，大海是多麼壯麗！

聽！海螺聲和鐘聲正在響起。

卡比爾說：「哦，兄弟，看！

神就坐在我的身體方舟中。」

II.48. jis se rahani apār jagat meṉ

MORE than all else do I cherish at heart that love which makes me to live a limitless life in this world.

It is like the lotus, which lives in the water and blooms in the water: yet the water cannot touch its petals, they open beyond its reach.

It is like a wife, who enters the fire at the bidding of love. She burns and lets others grieve, yet never dishonours love.

This ocean of the world is hard to cross: its waters are very deep.

Kabir says: "Listen to me, O Sadhu! few there are who have reached its end."

024

我用心珍惜這份愛，遠勝於一切，

這份愛讓我在這世界活出無限的生命。

它就像蓮花，在水中生長，在水中綻放：

而水無法觸及它的花瓣，它們開在水面之上。

就像一位妻子，她接受愛的邀請，步入火中。

她燃燒著，讓他人感到悲傷，

而她絕不將愛違背。

世界之海，難以橫渡：海水是如此深沉。

卡比爾說：「哦，苦行僧，請聽我說！

能抵達大海盡頭的人，少之又少。」

II. 45. Hari ne apnā āp chipāyā

MY Lord hides Himself, and my Lord wonder-
fully reveals Himself:
My Lord has encompassed me with hardness, and
my Lord has cast down my limitations.
My Lord brings to me words of sorrow and
words of joy, and He Himself heals their
strife.
I will offer my body and mind to my Lord: I will
give up my life, but never can I forget my
Lord!

025

真主將祂自己隱藏，
真主又神奇地顯現祂自己：
真主用艱辛將我包圍，
真主又將我的局限打破。
真主為我帶來噩耗和喜訊，
祂又親自療癒它們之間的衝突。
我將我的全身心奉獻給真主：
我願放棄我的生命，
但決不會將真主忘懷！

II.75. ōṇkār siwāe kōī sirjai

ALL things are created by the Om;

The love-form is His body.

He is without form, without quality, without decay:

Seek thou union with Him!

But that formless God takes a thousand forms in the
eyes of His creatures:

He is pure and indestructible,

His form is infinite and fathomless,

He dances in rapture, and waves of form arise from His
dance.

The body and the mind cannot contain themselves,
when they are touched by His great joy.

He is immersed in all consciousness, all joys, and all
sorrows;

He has no beginning and no end;

He holds all within His bliss.

026

萬物都由「唵」[15] 所創造；
愛的形式就是神的身體。
祂無形無質，永不朽壞：
那就尋求你與祂的合一！

但無形之神在祂的造物面前以千萬種形式顯現：
祂純粹而不可摧毀，
祂的形式無限而數不勝數，
祂在狂喜中舞蹈，形式之波從祂的舞步中升起。
當身心都被祂的極樂感動，它們將無法自持。
祂浸潤於一切意識、一切喜悅、一切悲哀之中；
祂無始無終；
祂讓一切都留在祂的福佑之中。

II.81. satgur sōī dayā kar dīnhā

IT is the mercy of my true Guru that has made
    me to know the unknown;
I have learned from Him how to walk without
    feet, to see without eyes, to hear without
    ears, to drink without mouth, to fly without
    wings;
I have brought my love and my meditation into
    the land where there is no sun and moon,
    nor day and night.
Without eating, I have tasted of the sweetness of
    nectar; and without water, I have quenched
    my thirst.
Where there is the response of delight, there is
    the fullness of joy. Before whom can that joy
    be uttered?
Kabir says: "The Guru is great beyond words, and
    great is the good fortune of the disciple."

027

正是我真正的古魯的仁慈，讓我知曉未知；

我已從祂那裡學會，

如何不用雙足而行、不用雙眼而看，

不用耳朵而聽，不用嘴唇而飲，不用翅膀而飛；

我已將我的愛和冥想帶到

沒有日月、沒有日夜的所在。

不食，我卻品嘗到甘露的甜蜜；

不飲，我卻已解除我的乾渴。

哪裡有快樂的回應，哪裡就有圓滿的喜悅。

我能向誰道出這樣的喜悅？

卡比爾說：「古魯的偉大，無以言喻，

古魯的弟子，又何其幸運！」

II.85. nirguṇ āge sarguṇ nācai

BEFORE the Unconditioned, the Conditioned
   dances:
"Thou and I are one!" this trumpet proclaims.
The Guru comes, and bows down before the
   disciple:
This is the greatest of wonders.

028

在無限面前，有限翩然起舞：

「你我本是一體！」小號手如此宣稱。

古魯前來，向弟子致敬：

這是最偉大的奇蹟。

II.87. Kabir kab se bhaye vairāgī

GORAKHNATH asks Kabir:

"Tell me, O Kabir, when did your vocation begin? Where did your love have its rise?"

Kabir answers:

"When He whose forms are manifold had not begun His play; when there was no Guru, and no disciple; when the world was not spread out; when the Supreme One was alone——

Then I became an ascetic; then, O Gorakh, my love was drawn to Brahma.

Brahma did not hold the crown on his head; the god Vishnu was not anointed as king; the power of Shiva was still unborn; when I was instructed in Yoga.

029

郭拉洽 [16] 問卡比爾：

「哦，卡比爾，告訴我，

從何時起，你聽到召喚？

你的愛又在哪裡升起？」

卡比爾答道：「當祂的形式多種多樣、

但祂的遊戲還沒開始之時；

當還沒有古魯、也沒有弟子之時；

當世界還沒有展開之時；

當至高者單獨之時——

然後，我成了一名苦修者；

哦，郭拉洽，然後我的愛被梵天吸引。

當時梵天沒有頭戴冠冕；

毗濕奴也沒有被封為王；

濕婆的神力還沒有誕生；

就在那時，我受到瑜伽指引。

I became suddenly revealed in Benares, and
    Ramananda illumined me;
I brought with me the thirst for the Infinite, and
    I have come for the meeting with Him.
In simplicity will I unite with the Simple One;
    my love will surge up.
O Gorakh, march thou with His music!"

在貝拿勒斯 [17]，我突然得到揭示，

同時拉瑪南達 [18] 啟蒙了我；

我升起對無限的渴望，

我來是為了與祂相見。

在簡單中，我將與至簡者合一；

我的愛將澎湃洶湧。

哦，郭拉洽，隨著祂的音樂，前行！」

II.95. yā tarvar meṉ ek pakherū

ON this tree is a bird: it dances in the joy of life.

None knows where it is: and who knows what
the burden of its music may be?

Where the branches throw a deep shade, there
does it have its nest: and it comes in the
evening and flies away in the morning, and
says not a word of that which it means.

None tell me of this bird that sings within me.

It is neither coloured nor colourless; it has
neither form nor outline;

It sits in the shadow of love.

It dwells within the Unattainable, the Infinite,
and the Eternal; and no one marks when it
comes and goes.

Kabir says: "O brother Sadhu! deep is the
mystery. Let wise men seek to know where
rests that bird."

030

在這棵樹上有一隻鳥：

牠在生命的喜悅中舞蹈。

沒有人知道牠身在何處：

誰又知道牠的音樂會是什麼樣的負荷？

樹枝在哪裡投下樹蔭，牠就在哪裡築巢：

牠暮至朝辭，對牠的來意，不置一詞。

沒有人向我提及

在我心中鳴唱的這隻鳥。

牠既不繽紛，也不黯淡；無形也無邊；

牠棲息於愛的陰影中。

牠居於不可及之處、無限之地、永恆之所；

沒有人能說出，牠何時到來，何時離開。

卡比爾說：「哦，苦行僧兄弟！

這神祕深不可測，

就讓智者找出這鳥兒的居所。」

卡比爾之歌

II.100. niś din sālai ghāw

A SORE pain troubles me day and night, and I
   cannot sleep;
I long for the meeting with my Beloved, and my
   father's house gives me pleasure no more.

The gates of the sky are opened, the temple is
   revealed:
I meet my husband, and leave at His feet the
   offering of my body and my mind.

031

有一種劇痛日夜折磨著我，
讓我無法入眠；
我渴望與我的摯愛相見，
我父親的家不再讓我滿足。

天門已經打開，神殿已經揭開；
我與我的夫君相見，
我要將我的身心奉獻在祂的跟前。

II.103. nāco re mero man, matta hoy

DANCE, my heart! dance to-day with joy.

The strains of love fill the days and the nights
with music, and the world is listening to its
melodies:

Mad with joy, life and death dance to the rhythm
of this music. The hills and the sea and the
earth dance. The world of man dances in
laughter and tears.

Why put on the robe of the monk, and live aloof
from the world in lonely pride?

Behold! my heart dances in the delight of a
hundred arts; and the Creator is well pleased.

032

我的心，起舞吧！
今天，懷著喜悅舞蹈。
愛的潮水用音樂充滿每日每夜，
世界正在聆聽它的旋律：
因喜悅而瘋狂，生與死和著這旋律起舞。
高山、海洋和大地一起起舞。
世人都在歡笑和淚水中起舞。
為何穿上僧袍，遠離塵世，
在孤獨和驕傲中生活？
看！我的心因喜悅而曼妙起舞；
造物主因我而無比歡喜。

II.105. man mast huā tab kyoṉ bole

WHERE is the need of words, when love has
made drunken the heart?

I have wrapped the diamond in my cloak; why
open it again and again?

When its load was light, the pan of the balance
went up; now it is full, where is the need for
weighing?

The swan has taken its flight to the lake beyond
the mountains; why should it search for the
pools and ditches any more?

Your Lord dwells within you; why need your
outward eyes be opened?

Kabir says: "Listen, my brother! my Lord, who
ravishes my eyes, has united Himself with
me."

033

當愛已讓心兒沉醉，還需言語？

我已將鑽石包裹在我的斗篷裡；

為何還要一再將它打開？

當負重輕鬆，秤盤就會翹起；

如今它已滿載，何需再去秤量？

天鵝已飛往山外的湖泊；

牠為何還要再尋找沼澤池塘？

真主就住在你心中；

為何你還在向外張望？

卡比爾說：「我的兄弟，聽好！

真主使我陶醉其中，祂已與我合一。」

II.110. mohi tohi lāgī kaise chuṭe

How could the love between Thee and me sever?

As the leaf of the lotus abides on the water: so
    thou art my Lord, and I am Thy servant.

As the night-bird Chakor gazes all night at the
    moon: so Thou art my Lord and I am Thy
    servant.

From the beginning until the ending of time,
    there is love between Thee and me; and how
    shall such love be extinguished?

Kabir says: "As the river enters into the ocean, so
    my heart touches Thee."

034

你與我之間的愛如何能分裂？
就像荷葉浮在水面：
你是我的真主，我是你的僕人。
就像夜鳥整夜凝望月亮：
你是我的真主，我是你的僕人。
你與我之間的愛，
自時間之始，延伸至時間的盡頭；
這樣的愛怎會熄滅？
卡比爾說：「就像河流匯入海洋，
我的心也將與你相會。」

II.113. vālam, āwo hamāre geh re

MY body and my mind are grieved for the want
of Thee;
O my Beloved! come to my house.
When people say I am Thy bride, I am ashamed;
for I have not touched Thy heart with my
heart.
Then what is this love of mine? I have no taste
for food, I have no sleep; my heart is ever
restless within doors and without.
As water is to the thirsty, so is the lover to the
bride. Who is there that will carry my news
to my Beloved?
Kabir is restless, he is dying for sight of Him.

035

因為對你的渴望，我的身心陷入悲傷；

哦，我的摯愛！請來到我的家中。

人們說，我就是你的新娘，

我感到羞愧難當；

因為我還沒有與你心相印。

那麼我的這份愛又是什麼？

我食不知味，我夜不能眠；

無論待在家裡還是出外，我的心依然惴惴不安。

戀人之於新娘，

正如水之於乾渴。

誰能將我的消息捎給我的摯愛？

卡比爾心神不安，他多麼渴望見到袖。

II.126. jāg piyārī, ab kān sowai

O FRIEND, awake, and sleep no more!

The night is over and gone, would you lose your
day also?

Others, who have wakened, have received jewels;

O foolish woman! you have lost all whilst you
slept.

Your lover is wise, and you are foolish, O woman!

You never prepared the bed of your husband:

O mad one! you passed your time in silly play.

Your youth was passed in vain, for you did not
know your Lord;

Wake, wake! See! your bed is empty: He left you
in the night.

Kabir says: "Only she wakes, whose heart is
pierced with the arrow of His music."

036

哦，朋友，醒來，別再睡去！
長夜已盡，難道你還要失去白日？
已經醒來的人，他們已得到珍寶；
哦，愚笨的婦人！
在你沉睡之時，你已失去所有。
你的、睿智，而你愚笨，哦，婦人！
你從不曾為你的夫君鋪床疊被：
哦，愚笨之人！你用愚蠢的遊戲虛度光陰。
你的青春已蹉跎，因為你認不出你的真主；
醒來，醒來！看！你的床上空空如也：
祂已在夜裡離你而去。
卡比爾說：「只有當她醒來，
她的心才會被祂的音樂之箭射中。」

I.36. sūr parkāś, tāṇh rain kahāṇ pāiye

WHERE is the night, when the sun is shining? If
it is night, then the sun withdraws its light.

Where knowledge is, can ignorance endure? If
there be ignorance, then knowledge must
die.

If there be lust, how can love be there? Where
there is love, there is no lust.

Lay hold on your sword, and join in the fight.
Fight, O my brother, as long as life lasts.

Strike off your enemy's head, and there make an
end of him quickly: then come, and bow
your head at your King's Durbar.

He who is brave, never forsakes the battle; he
who flies from it is no true fighter.

037

當陽光明媚，黑夜去往何方？

如果黑夜來臨，太陽就會收回它的光芒。

無知能否容身於知識的所在？

如果無知顯現，知識就會死亡。

如果有了貪慾，心中怎會有愛？

哪裡有愛，哪裡就沒有貪婪。

緊握你的利劍，加入戰鬥。

哦，我的兄弟，戰鬥，只要一息尚存。

砍下敵人的頭顱，一刀斃命：

然後來到國王的宮廷叩首拜見。

勇士，絕不會放棄戰鬥；

臨陣脫逃之人，不是真正的戰士。

In the field of this body a great war goes forward,
    against passion, anger, pride, and greed:
It is in the kingdom of truth, contentment and
    purity, that this battle is raging; and the
    sword that rings forth most loudly is the
    sword of His Name.
Kabir says: "When a brave knight takes the field,
    a host of cowards is put to flight.
It is a hard fight and a weary one, this fight of
    the truth-seeker: for the vow of the truth-
    seeker is more hard than that of the warrior,
    or of the widowed wife who would follow
    her husband.
For the warrior fights for a few hours, and the
    widow's struggle with death is soon ended;
But the truth-seeker's battle goes on day and
    night, as long as life lasts it never ceases."

在這身體的戰場上，一場大戰正在進行，

與激情、憤怒、驕傲和貪婪奮戰：

在真理、滿足和純粹的王國，激戰正酣；

神之名的利劍，發出最嘹亮的劍鳴。

卡比爾說：「沙場上一名勇士，

就能讓成群的懦夫聞風逃匿。

這是一場苦戰，這是真理尋求者之戰：

因為他的誓言難於戰士的誓言、

或寡婦殉葬的誓言。

因為戰士的戰鬥只延續幾個時辰，

寡婦很快就敵不過死神；

但真理尋求者之戰日以繼夜，

只要生命不息，戰鬥就不會停止。」

I.50. bhram kā tālā lagā mahal re

THE lock of error shuts the gate, open it with
the key of love:
Thus, by opening the door, thou shalt wake the
Beloved.
Kabir says: "O brother! do not pass by such good
fortune as this."

038

錯誤之鎖將大門緊鎖，
你要用愛的鑰匙將它開啟：
把門打開，你就會喚醒摯愛。
卡比爾說：「哦，兄弟！
如此好的運氣，豈容錯過。」

I.59. sādho, yah tan ṭhāṭh taṇvure kā

O FRIEND! this body is His lyre;

He tightens its strings, and draws from it the
melody of Brahma.

If the strings snap and the keys slacken, then to
dust must this instrument of dust return:

Kabir says: "None but Brahma can evoke its
melodies."

039

哦，朋友！這身體是祂的七弦琴；
祂調緊琴弦，彈奏梵天的妙音。
如果琴弦突然斷裂，琴鈕突然鬆脫，
這具塵土的樂器就必定回到塵土：
卡比爾說：「除了梵天，無人能將它彈奏。」

I.65. avadhū bhūle ko ghar lāwe

HE is dear to me indeed who can call back the wanderer to his home. In the home is the true union, in the home is enjoyment of life: why should I forsake my home and wander in the forest? If Brahma helps me to realize truth, verily I will find both bondage and deliverance in home.

He is dear to me indeed who has power to dive deep into Brahma; whose mind loses itself with ease in His contemplation.

He is dear to me who knows Brahma, and can dwell on His supreme truth in meditation; and who can play the melody of the Infinite by uniting love and renunciation in life.

Kabir says: "The home is the abiding place; in the home is reality; the home helps to attain Him Who is real. So stay where you are, and all things shall come to you in time."

040

他能將流浪者喚回他的家中，

他讓我感到如此可親。

回到家中，就是真正的合一，

回到家中，就是生命的享樂：

為何我要離家出走，在林中流浪？

如果梵天助我了知真理，

我就一定會在家中找出束縛和解脫。

他具有深入梵天的力量；

他在沉思中輕易地讓心智消融，

他讓我感到如此可親。

他知曉梵天，在靜心中安住於祂至高的真理；

他結合了生命之愛與解脫，奏響無限妙音，

他讓我感到如此可親。

卡比爾說：「家就是住所；家就是真實；

家幫助你找到真神。所以，待在你所在之處，

一切都會適時而至。」

I.76. santo, sahaj samādh bhalī

O SADHU! the simple union is the best.

Since the day when I met with my Lord, there
has been no end to the sport of our love.

I shut not my eyes, I close not my ears, I do not
mortify my body;

I see with eyes open and smile, and behold His
beauty everywhere:

I utter His Name, and whatever I see, it reminds
me of Him; whatever I do, it becomes His
worship.

The rising and the setting are one to me; all
contradictions are solved.

Wherever I go, I move round Him,

All I achieve is His service:

When I lie down, I lie prostrate at His feet.

He is the only adorable one to me: I have none
other.

Songs of Kabir

041

哦，苦行僧！單純的合一最佳。

從我遇見真主的那天起，

我們愛的遊戲就不曾終止。

我不閉上眼睛，我不堵住耳朵，

我不克制我的身體；

我睜開雙眼，張望微笑，看見祂的美無處不在：

我說出祂的名字，無論看見什麼，都讓我想起祂；

無論我做什麼，都變成對祂的禮拜。

於我而言，日升和日落沒有分別；

所有的矛盾都已消解。

無論我去哪裡，我都伴隨祂而行，

我所有的成就，都是祂的功勞；

當我躺下，我俯臥在祂的足前。

祂是我唯一崇拜的神：此外再無其他。

My tongue has left off impure words, it sings His
glory day and night.

Whether I rise or sit down, I can never forget
Him; for the rhythm of His music beats in
my ears.

Kabir says: "My heart is frenzied, and I disclose
in my soul what is hidden. I am immersed
in that one great bliss which transcends all
pleasure and pain."

我的口中不再說出不淨的言辭，

而是日夜歌唱祂的榮耀。

無論我站立還是坐下，我都無法將祂忘懷；

因為祂的樂音總是縈繞我的耳際。

卡比爾說：「我的心多麼狂熱，

我將靈魂中深藏的一切展露。

我浸淫在極度的福佑之中，

超越了一切歡樂苦痛。」

I.79. tīrath men̠ to sab pānī hai

THERE is nothing but water at the holy bathing
    places; and I know that they are useless, for I
    have bathed in them.
The images are all lifeless, they cannot speak; I
    know, for I have cried aloud to them.
The Purana and the Koran are mere words;
    lifting up the curtain, I have seen.
Kabir gives utterance to the words of experience;
    and he knows very well that all other things
    are untrue.

042

在神聖的沐浴之所，只有水；

我知道這沐浴之所毫無用處，

因為我已沐浴其中。

偶像都沒有生命，它們一言不發；

我知道，因為我曾向它們哭喊過。

《往世書》[19] 和《古蘭經》只是文字；

我已揭開布幕，我已看見。

卡比爾出自經驗發言；

他深知：其他的一切皆非真實。

I.82. pānī vic mīn piyāsī

I LAUGH when I hear that the fish in the water
is thirsty:
You do not see that the Real is in your home,
and you wander from forest to forest
listlessly!
Here is the truth! Go where you will, to Benares
or to Mathura; if you do not find your soul,
the world is unreal to you.

043

當我聽說，水中的魚兒會口渴，我放聲大笑：
你沒有看見，真實就在你的家中，
你卻無精打采地從一座森林徘徊到另一座森林！
真相就在此！
你可以去到任何地方，
無論是貝拿勒斯，還是馬圖拉[20]；
如果你還沒有發現你的靈魂，
整個世界於你而言都不真實。

I.93. gagan maṭh gaib nisān gaḍe

THE Hidden Banner is planted in the temple
of the sky; there the blue canopy decked
with the moon and set with bright jewels is
spread.

There the light of the sun and the moon is
shining: still your mind to silence before that
splendour.

Kabir says: "He who has drunk of this nectar,
wanders like one who is mad."

044

隱藏的旗幟插在天空的廟宇；

藍色的天穹鑲嵌著月亮並灑落著寶石般的明星。

日月之光在照耀：

面對這壯麗景象，讓你的心沉默安靜。

卡比爾說：「飲下這甘霖，

他會像是狂熱般漫遊。」

I.97. sādho, ko hai kānh se āyo

WHO are you, and whence do you come?

Where dwells that Supreme Spirit, and how does
He have His sport with all created things?

The fire is in the wood; but who awakens it
suddenly? Then it turns to ashes, and where
goes the force of the fire?

The true guru teaches that He has neither limit
nor infinitude.

Kabir says: "Brahma suits His language to the
understanding of His hearer."

045

你是誰？你來自哪裡？

至高靈性住在哪裡？

祂讓祂所有的造物如何遊戲？

火在柴禾之中；

但是誰突然將它喚醒？

當它化為灰燼，

火的力量又去往哪裡？

真正的古魯會如此教誨：

祂既非有限亦非無限。

卡比爾說：「梵天的語言

正好能讓祂的傾聽者了解。」

I.98. sādho, sahajai kāyā śodho

O SADHU ! purify your body in the simple way.

As the seed is within the banyan tree, and within
    the seed are the flowers, the fruits, and the
    shade:

So the germ is within the body, and within that
    germ is the body again.

The fire, the air, the water, the earth, and the
    aether; you cannot have these outside of Him.

O Kazi, O Pundit, consider it well: what is there
    that is not in the soul?

The water-filled pitcher is placed upon water, it
    has water within and without.

It should not be given a name, lest it call forth
    the error of dualism.

Kabir says: "Listen to the Word, the Truth, which
    is your essence. He speaks the Word to
    Himself; and He Himself is the Creator."

046

哦，苦行僧！以簡單之道淨化你的身體。

正如種子就在菩提樹裡，

種子裡也包含了花朵、果實和樹蔭：

細胞就在身體之中，

在這細胞之中又有身體。

火、風、水、地、空；你無法在祂之外找到它們。

哦，經學家，哦，梵學家，細細思量：

不在靈魂之中的是什麼？

將裝滿水的水罐放入水中，它的內外都是水。

不要給出名字，以免犯下二元論的錯誤。

卡比爾說：「聆聽音流，聆聽真理，

它就是你的本質。

祂對祂自己說出音流；

祂自己就是造物主。」

I.102. tarvar ek mūl bin ṭhāḍā

THERE is a strange tree, which stands without
roots and bears fruits without blossoming;
It has no branches and no leaves, it is lotus all
over.
Two birds sing there; one is the Guru, and the
other the disciple:
The disciple chooses the manifold fruits of life
and tastes them, and the Guru beholds him
in joy.
What Kabir says is hard to understand: "The
bird is beyond seeking, yet it is most clearly
visible. The Formless is in the midst of all
forms. I sing the glory of forms."

047

一棵奇異之樹，它無根而立，不花而果；
它無枝無葉，它是無處不在的蓮花。
兩隻鳥兒在那裡歌唱；
一隻是古魯，另一隻是門徒：
門徒選擇生命的種種果實，一一品嘗，
古魯愉快地看著他。
卡比爾所說的很難理解：
「這隻鳥兒無法找到，卻又最容易看見。
無形在所有有形之中。我歌頌有形的榮耀。」

I.107. calat mansā acal kīnhī

I HAVE stilled my restless mind, and my heart is
   radiant: for in Thatness I have seen beyond
   Thatness, in company I have seen the
   Comrade Himself.
Living in bondage, I have set myself free: I
   have broken away from the clutch of all
   narrowness.
Kabir says: "I have attained the unattainable, and
   my heart is coloured with the colour of
   love."

048

我已讓我不安的心念止息，
我的心放射光芒：
因為在彼之中，我已看到彼之外。
在陪伴之中，我已看到伴侶本人。
在束縛中生活，我已解脫自己：
我已掙脫一切狹隘的緊握。
卡比爾說：「我已達到無法達到的，
我的心已染上愛的色彩。」

卡比爾之歌

I.105. jo dīsai, so to hai nāhī̠ṉ

THAT which you see is not: and for that which
is, you have no words.

Unless you see, you believe not: what is told you
you cannot accept.

He who is discerning knows by the word; and
the ignorant stands gaping.

Some contemplate the Formless, and others
meditate on form: but the wise man knows
that Brahma is beyond both.

That beauty of His is not seen of the eye; that
metre of His is not heard of the ear.

Kabir says: "He who has found both love and
renunciation never descends to death."

049

它不是你所見：你也無法將它道出。

除非你親身看見，否則你不會相信：

別人告訴你的，你不會接受。

智者憑音流而知曉；

無知者卻站在那裡打哈欠。

有人沉思無形，有人冥想有形：

但智者知道，梵天超越兩者。

梵天之美，眼所不能見；

梵天之韻，耳所不能聞。

卡比爾說：「已經找到愛和解脫之人，

永遠不會沉淪在死亡裡。」

I.126. muralī bajat akhaṇḍ sadāye

THE flute of the Infinite is played without
    ceasing, and its sound is love:
When love renounces all limits, it reaches truth.
How widely the fragrance spreads! It has no end,
    nothing stands in its way.
The form of this melody is bright like a million
    suns: incomparably sounds the vina, the vina
    of the notes of truth.

050

無限之笛不停地吹奏著，愛就是它的樂音：
當愛擺脫所有限制，它就抵達真理。
這芬芳散播得多麼遼遠！
它沒有窮盡，沒有什麼能阻擋它的道路。
這悅耳的旋律像千萬顆太陽般明亮：
七弦琴奏出真理的音符，無可比擬。

I.129. sakhiyo, ham hūṉ bhāī vālamāśī

DEAR friend, I am eager to meet my Beloved!
My youth has flowered, and the pain of
separation from Him troubles my breast.
I am wandering yet in the alleys of knowledge
without purpose, but I have received His
news in these alleys of knowledge.
I have a letter from my Beloved: in this letter is
an unutterable message, and now my fear of
death is done away.
Kabir says: "O my loving friend! I have got for
my gift the Deathless One."

051

親愛的朋友，我急切地渴望與我的摯愛相見！

我的青春盛放，與衪的分離之苦折磨著我的心。

然而我依舊漫無目的地徘徊在知識的街巷，

但在這些知識的街巷，我已聽到有關衪的消息。

摯愛給我捎來一封信：

信中有一條無法言說的訊息，

而如今我已不再懼怕死亡。

卡比爾說：「哦，我心愛的朋友！

我已經得到了永恆不朽這一禮物。」

I.130. sāīn̲ bin dard kareje hoy

WHEN I am parted from my Beloved, my heart
is full of misery: I have no comfort in the
day, I have no sleep in the night. To whom
shall I tell my sorrow?

The night is dark; the hours slip by. Because my
Lord is absent, I start up and tremble with
fear.

Kabir says: "Listen, my friend! there is no other
satisfaction, save in the encounter with the
Beloved."

052

當與我的摯愛分離，

我的心中充滿痛苦：

白天，我不得安寧，

夜裡，我難以入眠。

我要向誰述說我的悲哀？

夜已深，時光流逝。

因為真主不在這裡，

我開始因恐懼而顫慄。

卡比爾說：「聽好，我的朋友！

除了與摯愛相遇，

再沒有其他任何滿足。」

I.122. kaun muralī śabd śun ānand bhayo

WHAT is that flute whose music thrills me with
    joy?
The flame burns without a lamp;
The lotus blossoms without a root;
Flowers bloom in clusters;
The moon-bird is devoted to the moon;
With all its heart the rain-bird longs for the
    shower of rain;
But upon whose love does the Lover concentrate
    His entire life?

053

那是一支什麼樣的笛子，

它的音樂讓我因喜悅而顫慄？

燭火燃燒，而無需燈盞；

蓮花綻放，而無需根鬚；

繁花盛開；

月鳥獻身於月亮；

雨燕滿心渴望一場大雨；

可是，摯愛用祂整個生命傾注於誰的愛？

I.112. śuntā nahī dhun kī khabar

HAVE you not heard the tune which the Unstruck Music is playing? In the midst of the chamber the harp of joy is gently and sweetly played; and where is the need of going without to hear it?

If you have not drunk of the nectar of that One Love, what boots it though you should purge yourself of all stains?

The Kazi is searching the words of the Koran, and instructing others; but if his heart be not steeped in that love, what does it avail, though he be a teacher of men?

The Yogi dyes his garments with red; but if he knows naught of that colour of love, what does it avail though his garments be tinted?

054

你還從未聽過不奏自響的音樂？

歡樂的豎琴輕柔甜美地在室內奏響；

想要聆聽，又何需外出？

如果你還沒有啜飲

合一之愛的甘露，

即使洗淨了全身的污跡，

這又有何用？

經學家翻閱《古蘭經》，將經文傳授給他人；

但如果他的心沒有浸潤在這愛之中，

即使身為人師，

這又有何用？

瑜伽行者把他的衣裳染紅；

但如果他還不知曉愛的色彩，

即使衣服染上了顏色，

這又有何用？

Kabir says: "Whether I be in the temple or the
balcony, in the camp or in the flower garden,
I tell you truly that every moment my Lord
is taking His delight in me."

卡比爾說：「無論我身處廟宇還是陽台，

在營地還是在花園，

我都把實話告訴你：

每一刻，我的心中都充滿真主的愉悅歡欣。」

I.73. bhakti kā mārag jhīnā re

SUBTLE is the path of love!

Therein there is no asking and no not-asking,

There one loses one's self at His feet,

There one is immersed in the joy of the seeking:

    plunged in the deeps of love as the fish in

    the water.

The lover is never slow in offering his head for

    his Lord's service.

Kabir declares the secret of this love.

055

愛的道路多麼奧妙！
在那裡，沒有提問，也沒有不問，
在祂的跟前，一個人會失去自我，
在那裡，一個人會沉浸在尋求的喜悅中：
投入深深的愛之中，猶如魚兒入水。
戀人會毫不遲疑地服侍真主。
卡比爾為你揭示，這愛的祕密。

I.68. bhāī kōī satguru sant kahāwai

HE is the real Sadhu, who can reveal the form of
the Formless to the vision of these eyes;
Who teaches the simple way of attaining Him,
that is other than rites or ceremonies;
Who does not make you close the doors, and
hold the breath, and renounce the world;
Who makes you perceive the Supreme Spirit
wherever the mind attaches itself;
Who teaches you to be still in the midst of all
your activities.
Ever immersed in bliss, having no fear in his
mind, he keeps the spirit of union in the
midst of all enjoyments.
The infinite dwelling of the Infinite Being is
everywhere: in earth, water, sky, and air;

056

能將無形之形示現在人們眼前，

這樣的人是真正的苦行僧；

他能傳授找到神的簡單方法，

而非禮拜和儀式；

他不讓你把門緊閉，

也不要你屏住呼吸、棄世遠離；

他讓你認識至高靈性，

而無論你的心念在哪裡；

他教你在一切行動中保有寧靜。

永遠浸潤在至福之中，

他的心中沒有恐懼，

他在喜悅中體現合一的精神。

無限存在的無限居所無處不在：

在地上、在水裡、在天空、在風中；

Firm as the thunderbolt, the seat of the seeker is

established above the void.

He who is within is without: I see Him and none

else.

尋求者的座椅置於虛空之上，
像雷電一般堅定。
祂在內在，也在外在：
我只看見祂，別無其他。

I.66. sādho, śabd sādhanā kījai

RECEIVE that Word from which the Universe
   springeth!
That Word is the Guru; I have heard it, and
   become the disciple.
How many are there who know the meaning of
   that Word?

O Sadhu! practise that Word!
The Vedas and the Puranas proclaim it,
The world is established in it,
The Rishis and devotees speak of it:
But none knows the mystery of the Word.
The householder leaves his house when he hears it,
The ascetic comes back to love when he hears it,
The Six Philosophies expound it,

057

聆聽這音流，

宇宙源於其中！

這音流就是古魯；

我已聽到，

我已成為門徒。

有多少人知曉音流的真諦？

哦，苦行僧，修習這音流！

《吠陀經》和《往世書》把它宣講，

世界在它之中建立，

仙人和皈依者把它談論：

但無人知曉音流的祕密。

當居家者聽到音流，他就會離家，

當苦修者聽到音流，他就會回歸愛，

六大哲學將它闡述，

The Spirit of Renunciation points to that Word,

From that Word the world-form has sprung,

That Word reveals all.

Kabïr says: "But who knows whence the Word

    cometh?"

解脫之靈性指向音流，
有形的世界從音流中誕生，
音流揭示一切。
卡比爾說：「但有誰知道，
音流又來自何方？」

I.63. pī le pyālā, ho matwālā

EMPTY the Cup! O be drunken!

Drink the divine nectar of His Name!

Kabir says: "Listen to me, dear Sadhu!

From the sole of the foot to the crown of the
head this mind is filled with poison."

058

飲盡杯中酒！哦，一醉方休！
暢飲祂聖名的甘露！
卡比爾說：「請聽我說，親愛的苦行僧！
從頭頂到腳底，心智充滿了毒藥。」

I.52. khasm na cīnhai bāwarī

O MAN, if thou dost not know thine own Lord,
   whereof art thou so proud?
Put thy cleverness away: mere words shall never
   unite thee to Him.
Do not deceive thyself with the witness of the
   Scriptures:
Love is something other than this, and he who
   has sought it truly has found it.

059

哦，人啊，若你還不認識自己的真主，
又為何如此驕傲？
將你的聰明放下：
單憑言語，絕不會讓你與祂合一。
不要引經據典，欺騙自己：
愛和這些都不相同，
只有真正的尋求之人才會找到。

I.56. sukh sindh kī sair kā

THE savour of wandering in the ocean of
    deathless life has rid me of all my asking:
As the tree is in the seed, so all diseases are in
    this asking.

060

流浪在不死的生命之海裡，
這滋味已讓我放下一切追求：
正如大樹就在種子裡，
所有的病痛也都在這追求中。

I.48. sukh sāgar men āīke

WHEN at last you are come to the ocean of
   happiness, do not go back thirsty.
Wake, foolish man! for Death stalks you. Here
   is pure water before you; drink it at every
   breath.
Do not follow the mirage on foot, but thirst for
   the nectar;
Dhruva, Prahlad, and Shukadeva have drunk of it,
   and also Raidas has tasted it:
The saints are drunk with love, their thirst is for
   love.
Kabir says: "Listen to me, brother! The nest of
   fear is broken.
Not for a moment have you come face to face
   with the world:

061

當你最終抵達幸福的海洋，

你可不要口渴而返。

醒醒，愚蠢的人！

因為死神正在悄悄臨近。

清水就在你面前；

快暢飲，莫稍停。

不要追逐海市蜃樓，而要渴望這甘露；

德魯瓦、普拉哈德、蘇卡神已暢飲過它，

雷達斯也將它品嘗：

聖人因愛而醉，

他們的口渴是對愛的渴望。

卡比爾說：「兄弟，請聽我說！

恐懼的巢穴已經打破。

你還未真正面對世界，哪怕短暫一瞬：

You are weaving your bondage of falsehood, your words are full of deception:

With the load of desires which you hold on your head, how can you be light?"

Kabir says: "Keep within you truth, detachment, and love."

你在編織你虛偽的束縛，

你的話裡充滿欺騙；

頭頂著欲望的重負，你怎會輕鬆？」

卡比爾說：「將真理、解脫，

和愛留在你心中。」

I.35. satī ko kaun śikhāwtā hai

WHO has ever taught the widowed wife to burn
   herself on the pyre of her dead husband?
And who has ever taught love to find bliss in
   renunciation?

062

有誰曾教導寡婦，
為她死去的夫君
在火葬的柴堆上殉葬？
有誰曾教導愛
在解脫中找到至福？

I.39. are man, dhīraj kāhe na dharai

WHY so impatient, my heart ?

He who watches over birds, beasts, and insects,

He who cared for you whilst you were yet in
your mother's womb,

Shall He not care for you now that you are come
forth?

Oh my heart, how could you turn from the smile
of your Lord and wander so far from Him ?

You have left your Beloved and are thinking of
others: and this is why all your work is in
vain.

063

我的心兒，為何這般沒有耐心？
是祂看顧鳥獸和蟲蟻，
是祂關愛著你，當你還在母親的子宮裡。
如今你來到祂面前，祂怎會不將你眷顧？
哦，我的心兒，當真主微笑向你，
你怎能轉身徘徊，離祂如此遙遠？
你已經離開你的摯愛，心中想著別人：
這就是為何你所有努力都將徒勞。

卡比爾之歌

I.117. sāīṉ se lagan kaṭhin hai, bhāī

How hard it is to meet my Lord!

The rain-bird wails in thirst for the rain: almost
she dies of her longing, yet she would have
none other water than the rain.

Drawn by the love of music, the deer moves
forward: she dies as she listens to the music,
yet she shrinks not in fear.

The widowed wife sits by the body of her dead
husband: she is not afraid of the fire.

Put away all fear for this poor body.

064

如今，與真主相見是多麼艱難！

雨燕的悲歎是對大雨的渴望：

她幾乎因渴望而死，

除了雨之外，她不需要別的水。

受音樂之愛吸引，鹿兒一路向前：

當她聽到這音樂，她便死去，

但她不會因恐懼而顫慄。

寡婦坐在死去的丈夫身旁：

她並不懼怕火焰。

放下所有關於這粗陋身體的恐懼。

1
9
2
/
1
9
3

I.22. jab main bhūlā, re bhāī

O BROTHER! when I was forgetful, my true
    Guru showed me the Way.
Then I left off all rites and ceremonies, I bathed
    no more in the holy water:
Then I learned that it was I alone who was mad,
    and the whole world beside me was sane;
    and I had disturbed these wise people.
From that time forth I knew no more how to
    roll in the dust in obeisance:
I do not ring the temple bell;
I do not set the idol on its throne;
I do not worship the image with flowers.

It is not the austerities that mortify the flesh
    which are pleasing to the Lord,

065

哦，兄弟！當我遺忘，
我真正的古魯就為我指出道路。
於是，我拋棄所有的禮拜和儀式，
我不再在聖水中沐浴：
於是，我明白發瘋的正是自己，
我周圍的整個世界都很清醒；
是我打擾了這些智者。
從此，我不再知道
如何在塵世中恭敬地過活：
我不再敲響廟鐘；
我不再將偶像置於神座；
我不再用鮮花供奉神像。

克制肉欲的苦行並不能取悅真主，

When you leave off your clothes and kill your
senses, you do not please the Lord.

The man who is kind and who practises righ-
teousness, who remains passive amidst
the affairs of the world, who considers all
creatures on earth as his own self,

He attains the Immortal Being, the true God is
ever with him.

Kabir says: "He attains the true Name whose
words are pure, and who is free from pride
and conceit."

當你脫去衣服，扼殺你的感官，
你並沒有愉悅真主。
善良的人，正直的人，
不為世事所擾的人，視眾生為自己的人，
他來到了不朽之存在，
真神永遠在他心中。
卡比爾說：「當他得知了真名，
他的話語變得純淨，
他不再傲慢狂妄。」

I.20. man na raṅgāye

THE Yogi dyes his garments, instead of dyeing
his mind in the colours of love:
He sits within the temple of the Lord, leaving
Brahma to worship a stone.
He pierces holes in his ears, he has a great beard
and matted locks, he looks like a goat:
He goes forth into the wilderness, killing all his
desires, and turns himself into an eunuch.
He shaves his head and dyes his garments; he
reads the Gita and becomes a mighty talker.
Kabir says: "You are going to the doors of death,
bound hand and foot!"

066

瑜伽行者將他的衣服染色，

而不是將他的思想染上愛的顏色：

他坐在真主的廟宇中，

離開梵天，而去崇拜一塊石頭。

他在耳朵打上耳洞，他蓄著亂蓬蓬的鬍子，

他看上去像一頭山羊：

他變得瘋狂，扼殺自己所有的欲望，

把自己變成了閹人。

他把頭髮剃光，把衣服染色；

他閱讀《薄伽梵歌》，變得能說會道。

卡比爾說：「你正在走向死亡之門，

把自己的手腳牢牢捆綁！」

I.9. nā jāne sāhab kaisā hai

I DO not know what manner of God is mine.

The Mullah cries aloud to Him: and why? Is
 your Lord deaf? The subtle anklets that ring
 on the feet of an insect when it moves are
 heard of Him.

Tell your beads, paint your forehead with the
 mark of your God, and wear matted locks
 long and showy: but a deadly weapon is in
 your heart, and how shall you have God?

067

我不知道我的神是什麼樣子。

毛拉對他的神大喊大叫：

這是為什麼？你的真主聾了嗎？

一隻昆蟲爬行時，足上精巧的踝環發出輕響，

神也一樣會聽到。

默數你的念珠，

在你的額頭畫上神的記號，

同時蓄著長長的髮辮：

但這個致命的武器就在你心中，

你又如何能擁有神？

2001 / 2001

卡比爾之歌

III.102. ham se rahā na jāy

I HEAR the melody of His flute, and I cannot
    contain myself:
The flower blooms, though it is not spring; and
    already the bee has received its invitation.
The sky roars and the lightning flashes, the waves
    arise in my heart,
The rain falls; and my heart longs for my Lord.
Where the rhythm of the world rises and falls,
    thither my heart has reached:
There the hidden banners are fluttering in the
    air.
Kabir says: "My heart is dying, though it lives."

068

當我聽到祂的笛子吹奏美妙的旋律，我不能自已：

花兒綻放，儘管現在不是春天；

蜜蜂已經收到邀請。

天空發出怒號，電閃雷鳴，

我心中波濤洶湧。

大雨傾盆；我的心渴望真主。

世界的節奏在哪裡起伏，

我的心就來到哪裡：

隱藏的旗幟在空中招展。

卡比爾說：「我的心即將死去，

儘管它尚存一息。」

III.2. jo khodā masjid vasat hai

IF God be within the mosque, then to whom
    does this world belong?
If Ram be within the image which you find
    upon your pilgrimage, then who is there to
    know what happens without ?
Hari is in the East; Allah is in the West. Look
    within your heart, for there you will find
    both Karim and Ram;
All the men and women of the world are His
    living forms.
Kabir is the child of Allah and of Ram: He is my
    Guru, He is my Pir.

069

如果神在清真寺裡，那麼這個世界又屬於誰？

如果拉姆神就在你朝聖時看見的偶像裡，

那麼又是誰了知外面發生的事？

訶利在東方；安拉在西方。

注視你的內心，因為在那裡

你會找到卡利姆神和拉姆神；

這個世界的所有男人和女人

都是祂活生生的形象。

卡比爾是安拉和拉姆神之子：

祂是我的古魯，祂是我的聖人。

III.9. śīl santosh sadā samadṛishṭi

HE who is meek and contented, he who has an
equal vision, whose mind is filled with the
fullness of acceptance and of rest;

He who has seen Him and touched Him, he is
freed from all fear and trouble.

To him the perpetual thought of God is like
sandal paste smeared on the body, to him
nothing else is delight:

His work and his rest are filled with music; he
sheds abroad the radiance of love.

Kabir says: "Touch His feet, who is one and
indivisible, immutable and peaceful; who fills
all vessels to the brim with joy, and whose
form is love."

070

他謙卑而滿足，他有著平等心，

他全然接納，安住於心；

他已看見祂，他已觸及祂，

他解脫了所有恐懼煩憂。

對他而言，神的永恆觀念就像塗在身上的檀香，

對他而言，再沒有別的什麼歡愉：

他的工作和休息都充滿音樂；

他散發著愛的光芒。

卡比爾說：「觸摸祂的腳，

祂是一、不可分、不改變、平靜安寧；

祂將喜悅盛滿所有容器，

祂的形體就是愛。」

III.13. sādh saṅgat pītam

GO thou to the company of the good, where the
   Beloved One has His dwelling place:
Take all thy thoughts and love and instruction
   from thence.
Let that assembly be burnt to ashes where His
   Name is not spoken!
Tell me, how couldst thou hold a wedding-feast,
   if the bridegroom himself were not there?
Waver no more, think only of the Beloved;
Set not thy heart on the worship of other gods,
   there is no worth in the worship of other
   masters.
Kabir deliberates and says: "Thus thou shalt never
   find the Beloved!"

071

行事皆與美善為伴，那是摯愛的居所：

讓所有的心念、愛和指引皆由此而發。

讓不稱頌祂名字的集會之地燒成灰燼！

哦，告訴我，如果新郎缺席，你怎能舉行婚禮？

別再猶豫，一心想念摯愛；

不要讓你的心崇敬別的神，

別的大師也不值得崇拜。

卡比爾沉思良久，說道：

「因為那樣的話，你將永遠找不到摯愛！」

III.26. tor hīrā hirāilwā kīcaḍ meṉ

THE jewel is lost in the mud, and all are seeking for it;

Some look for it in the east, and some in the west; some in the water and some amongst stones.

But the servant Kabir has appraised it at its true value, and has wrapped it with care in the end of the mantle of his heart.

072

寶石落入泥潭，所有人都在尋找；

有人尋到東，有人找到西；

有人在水中尋找，有人在石堆裡尋找。

但僕人卡比爾識得它真正的價值，

小心地將它包裹，藏進他內心深處。

III.26. āyau din gaune kā ho

THE palanquin came to take me away to my
husband's home, and it sent through my
heart a thrill of joy;
But the bearers have brought me into the lonely
forest, where I have no one of my own.
O bearers, I entreat you by your feet, wait but
a moment longer: let me go back to my
kinsmen and friends, and take my leave of
them.
The servant Kabir sings: "O Sadhu! finish your
buying and selling, have done with your
good and your bad: for there are no markets
and no shops in the land to which you go."

073

轎子已來到我門前，要送我至夫君家，

我的心在喜悅中顫抖；

但轎夫將我抬進孤單的林中，我舉目無親。

哦，轎夫，我跪下來求你，

請再稍等片刻：

讓我回到我家人和親友那裡，

讓我向他們告別。

僕人卡比爾唱道：「哦，苦行僧！

結清你的買賣，了去你的善行和惡舉：

因為在你要去之地，

沒有市集，也沒有店鋪。」

III.30. are dil, prem nagar kā ant na pāyā

O MY heart! you have not known all the secrets
of this city of love: in ignorance you came,
and in ignorance you return.

O my friend, what have you done with this life?
You have taken on your head the burden
heavy with stones, and who is to lighten it
for you?

Your Friend stands on the other shore, but you
never think in your mind how you may
meet with Him:

The boat is broken, and yet you sit ever upon the
bank; and thus you are beaten to no purpose
by the waves.

The servant Kabir asks you to consider: who is
there that shall befriend you at the last?

You are alone, you have no companion: you will
suffer the consequences of your own deeds.

074

哦，我的心！

你還未瞭解這愛之城的全部祕密：

你無知地前來，你無知地離開。

哦，我的朋友，你都用這一生做了什麼？

你已在自己的頭頂壓上沉重的巨石，

誰來為你減輕負擔？

你的摯友站在對岸，

但你從未想過，要如何才能與祂相見：

船已朽壞，但你還坐在岸邊；

你被巨浪擊打，毫無緣由。

僕人卡比爾請你想一想：

到了最後，誰會與你為友？

你孤身一人，無人相伴：

你一切作為的後果，都要獨自承擔。

III.55. ved kahe sarguṇ ke āge

THE VEDAS say that the Unconditioned stands
   beyond the world of Conditions.

O woman, what does it avail thee to dispute
   whether He is beyond all or in all?

See thou everything as thine own dwelling place:
   the mist of pleasure and pain can never
   spread there.

There Brahma is revealed day and night: there
   light is His garment, light is His seat, light
   rests on thy head.

Kabir says: "The Master, who is true, He is all
   light."

075

《吠陀經》說：無限超越了有限的世界。

哦，婦人，你爭論

祂是在萬物之內、還是在萬物之外，

這又有什麼意義？

把萬物視作你自己的居所：

歡樂與痛苦的迷霧永遠無法在那裡彌漫。

在那裡，梵天日夜顯現：

在那裡，光明是祂的衣袍，光明是祂的座椅，

光明安歇於你的頭頂。

卡比爾說：「真正的主人，

祂就是一切光明。」

III.48. tū surat nain nihār

OPEN your eyes of love, and see Him who
    pervades this world! consider it well, and
    know that this is your own country.
When you meet the true Guru, He will awaken
    your heart;
He will tell you the secret of love and detach-
    ment, and then you will know indeed that
    He transcends this universe.
This world is the City of Truth, its maze of paths
    enchants the heart:
We can reach the goal without crossing the road,
    such is the sport unending.
Where the ring of manifold joys ever dances
    about Him, there is the sport of Eternal
    Bliss.

076

睜開你愛的雙眼，

看見祂遍布於這個世界，

細思量，了知這裡就是你的家鄉。

當你遇見真正的古魯，

祂會喚醒你的心；

祂會告訴你愛和超脫的祕密，

於是，你就會明白，祂超越了這宇宙。

這個世界是真理之城，

它的迷宮讓心感到迷惘：

我們不用跨上路就能抵達目的，

這條路是無休止的遊戲。

種種喜悅不斷圍繞著祂起舞，

那裡是永恆至福的遊戲。

When we know this, then all our receiving and
renouncing is over;
Thenceforth the heat of having shall never
scorch us more.

He is the Ultimate Rest unbounded:
He has spread His form of love throughout all
the world.
From that Ray which is Truth, streams of new
forms are perpetually springing: and He
pervades those forms.
All the gardens and groves and bowers are
abounding with blossom; and the air breaks
forth into ripples of joy.
There the swan plays a wonderful game,
There the Unstruck Music eddies around the
Infinite One;
There in the midst the Throne of the Unheld is
shining, whereon the great Being sits——

當我們明白這一點，

我們所有的獲取和丟棄都會終了；

從此，擁有的熱切不再將我們煎熬。

祂是無限自由的究竟安息：

祂將祂愛的形式遍滿世界。

自真理之光中，

新的形式不斷流出湧現：

祂遍滿於這些形式。

繁花盛開在所有的花園、樹林和涼亭；

喜悅的漣漪在空中蕩漾。

在那裡，天鵝玩著一個神奇的遊戲，

不奏自響的音樂環繞著無限之神；

無形無執的王座光芒閃耀，

偉大的存在端坐其上——

Millions of suns are shamed by the radiance of a single hair of His body.

On the harp of the road what true melodies are being sounded! and its notes pierce the heart:

There the Eternal Fountain is playing its endless life-streams of birth and death.

They call Him Emptiness who is the Truth of truths, in Whom all truths are stored!

There within Him creation goes forward, which is beyond all philosophy; for philosophy cannot attain to Him:

There is an endless world, O my Brother! and there is the Nameless Being, of whom nought can be said.

Only he knows it who has reached that region: it is other than all that is heard and said.

千萬個太陽抵不上祂一根毫髮的光芒。

一路上豎琴奏響著真實的旋律！

它的音符震撼心靈：

永恆之泉玩弄著生與死的無盡生命水流。

他們稱祂為空無，

祂是真理中的真理，

所有的真理都藏在其中！

在祂之中，創造一路向前，

超越所有哲學；

因為哲學無法觸及祂：

哦，我的兄弟！

有一個無限的世界，

那裡是無以名之的存在，

無法將祂道出。

只有來到這個領域的人才會明白：

這與所有你聽過和說過的都不相同。

No form, no body, no length, no breadth is seen
there: how can I tell you that which it is?

He comes to the Path of the Infinite on whom
the grace of the Lord descend: he is freed
from births and deaths who attains to Him.

Kabir says: "It cannot be told by the words of the
mouth, it cannot be written on paper:

It is like a dumb person who tastes a sweet
thing——how shall it be explained?"

在那裡，看不見形，看不見體，看不見邊際：

我如何才能向你描述那情形？

誰走上無限之路，

真主的恩典就會為他降臨：

他抵達神的所在，解脫了生死的束縛。

卡比爾說：「這無法用口說出，

也無法寫在紙上：

就像一個品嘗到甜蜜的啞巴——

這要如何向你形容？」

III.60. cal haṃsā wā deś jahāṉ

O MY heart! let us go to that country where
    dwells the Beloved, the ravisher of my heart!

There Love is filling her pitcher from the well,
    yet she has no rope wherewith to draw
    water;

There the clouds do not cover the sky, yet the
    rain falls down in gentle showers:

O bodiless one! do not sit on your doorstep; go
    forth and bathe yourself in that rain!

There it is ever moonlight and never dark; and
    who speaks of one sun only? that land is
    illuminate with the rays of a million suns.

077

哦，我的心！
讓我們前往摯愛居住的國度，
袛已攫取了我的心！
在那裡，愛將井水裝滿了她的水罐，
然而她不需要任何汲水的井繩；
在那裡，烏雲並未遮蔽天空，
然而依然下起了輕柔地陣雨。
哦，沒有肉身之人！不要坐在你的門口；
出來吧，讓自己沐浴在雨中！
在那裡，從來沒有黑暗，月光永遠照耀；
而誰說只有一個太陽？
大地被千萬顆太陽照亮。

III.63. kahaiṉ Kabīr, śuno ho sādho

KABIR says: "O Sadhu! hear my deathless words.
If you want your own good, examine and
consider them well.

You have estranged yourself from the Creator, of
whom you have sprung: you have lost your
reason, you have bought death.

All doctrines and all teachings are sprung from
Him, from Him they grow: know this for
certain, and have no fear.

Hear from me the tidings of this great truth!

Whose name do you sing, and on whom do
you meditate? O, come forth from this
entanglement!

He dwells at the heart of all things, so why take
refuge in empty desolation?

078

卡比爾說：「哦，苦行僧！

請聽我不朽之言。

如果你為自己著想，

那就將它細細思量。

你已疏遠了造物主，是祂將你創造；

你已失去了理智，你已接受死亡。

所有的教條和教義都源自於祂，

它們從祂那裡成長：

確實了知這一點，不帶恐懼。

從我這裡聆聽這偉大真理的潮音！

你歌唱誰的名字，你冥想誰？

哦，來吧，擺脫這糾纏！

祂居於萬物的心中，

你為何還躲在空虛的悲哀裡？

If you place the Guru at a distance from you,
then it is but the distance that you honour:
If indeed the Master be far away, then who is it
else that is creating this world?
When you think that He is not here, then you
wander further and further away, and seek
Him in vain with tears.
Where He is far off, there He is unattainable;
where He is near, He is very bliss.
Kabir says: "Lest His servant should suffer pain
He pervades him through and through."
Know yourself then, O Kabir; for He is in you
from head to foot.
Sing with gladness, and keep your seat unmoved
within your heart.

如果你讓古魯與你距離遙遠，

那麼你崇敬的只是這距離：

如果真主確實遠在天邊，

那麼還有誰來創造這個世界？

當你以為祂不在這裡，

那麼你就不斷徘徊越離越遠，

在哭泣中徒勞尋找。

當祂遠在天邊，就遙不可及；

當祂近在眼前，祂就是至福。

卡比爾說：「唯恐祂的僕人受苦，

祂讓自己遍滿遍在。」

哦，卡比爾，那就認識你自己；

因為祂就在你之中遍滿全身。

喜悅地歌唱，將你的座椅

牢牢地安置於心中。

III.66. nā maiṉ dharmī nahīṉ adharmī

I AM neither pious nor ungodly,

I live neither by law nor by sense,

I am neither a speaker nor hearer,

I am neither a servant nor master,

I am neither bond nor free,

I am neither detached nor attached.

I am far from none: I am near to none.

I shall go neither to hell nor to heaven.

I do all works; yet I am apart from all works.

Few comprehend my meaning: he who can comprehend it, he sits unmoved.

Kabir seeks neither to establish nor to destroy.

079

我既非不敬神，也非虔誠，

我既不依據律法生活，也不依賴感官。

我既非言說者，也非聆聽者，

我既非僕人，也非主人。

我既未被束縛，也非自由，

我既非無執，也非執著。

我既不遠離什麼，也不靠近什麼。

我既不前往地獄，也不前往天堂。

我做所有的工作，而我遠離所有的工作。

沒有幾人能理解我的意思：

如果誰能明白，他就會端坐不動。

卡比爾既不想建造，也不想破壞。

III.69. satta nām hai sab teṇ nyārā

THE true Name is like none other name!

The distinction of the Conditioned from the
Unconditioned is but a word:

The Unconditioned is the seed, the Conditioned
is the flower and the fruit.

Knowledge is the branch, and the Name is the
root.

Look, and see where the root is: happiness shall
be yours when you come to the root.

The root will lead you to the branch, the leaf,
the flower, and the fruit:

It is the encounter with the Lord, it is the attain-
ment of bliss, it is the reconciliation of the
Conditioned and the Unconditioned.

080

真名不同於其他任何名字！

有限與無限只有一字之差：

無限是種子，有限是它的花朵和果實。

知識是樹枝，真名是它的樹根。

看，瞧瞧樹根所在之處：

當你來到樹根，幸福就會屬於你。

樹根會帶你到樹枝、樹葉、花和果實：

這是與真主相遇，這是獲得至福，

這是有限與無限的和解。

III.74. pratham ek jo āpai āp

IN the beginning was He alone, sufficient
    unto Himself: the formless, colourless, and
    unconditioned Being.
Then was there neither beginning, middle, nor
    end;
Then were no eyes, no darkness, no light;
Then were no ground, air, nor sky; no fire, water,
    nor earth; no rivers like the Ganges and the
    Jumna, no seas, oceans, and waves.
Then was neither vice nor virtue; scriptures
    there were not, as the Vedas and Puranas, nor
    as the Koran.
Kabir ponders in his mind and says: "Then
    was there no activity: the Supreme Being
    remained merged in the unknown depths of
    His own self."

081

一開始祂獨一而自足：

無形、無色、無限的存在。

接著是無始、無終、也無中間；

接著是無眼界；無黑暗，無光亮；

接著是無地、無天、也無空氣；

無火、水、土；無河——

比如恆河與朱木納河，

無海，也無海浪。

接著是無善無惡；

無經文——比如《吠陀經》、《往世書》，

也沒有《古蘭經》。

卡比爾陷入沉思，說：

「然後沒有任何活動：

至高存在依然消沒於

祂自己未知的深度。」

The Guru neither eats nor drinks, neither lives
    nor dies:

Neither has He form, line, colour, nor vesture.

He who has neither caste nor clan nor anything
    else——how may I describe His glory ?

He has neither form nor formlessness,

He has no name,

He has neither colour nor colourlessness,

He has no dwelling-place.

古魯不吃不喝，不死也不活：

祂無形、無相、無色、無衣。

祂既沒有種姓，也沒有氏族，也沒有其他——

我如何才能描述祂的榮耀？

祂既非無形也非有形，祂無名，

祂既非無色也非有色，祂居於無處。

III.76. kahaiṉ Kabīr vicār ke

KABIR ponders and says: "He who has neither
caste nor country, who is formless and
without quality, fills all space."

The Creator brought into being the Game of Joy:
and from the word Om the Creation sprang.

The earth is His joy; His joy is the sky;

His joy is the flashing of the sun and the moon;

His joy is the beginning, the middle, and the end;

His joy is eyes, darkness, and light.

Oceans and waves are His joy: His joy the
Sarasvati, the Jumna, and the Ganges.

The Guru is One: and life and death, union and
separation, are all His plays of joy!

His play the land and water, the whole universe!

His play the earth and the sky!

082

卡比爾陷入沉思，說：

「祂既沒有種姓，也沒有家鄉，

祂無形、無質、充滿虛空。」

造物主創造了喜悅的遊戲；

創造從「唵」字中誕生。

大地是祂的喜悅；

祂的喜悅是天空；

祂的喜悅是日月的光芒；

祂的喜悅是開始、中間和終結；

祂的喜悅是眼界、黑暗和光明。

海洋和波浪是祂的喜悅：

祂的喜悅是薩拉斯瓦蒂河 [21]，是朱木納河與恆河。

古魯是一：生與死、合一與分離，

都是祂喜悅的遊戲！

祂的遊戲是土和水，整個宇宙！

祂的遊戲是天空和大地！

In play is the Creation spread out, in play it is established. The whole world, says Kabir, rests in His play, yet still the Player remains unknown.

創造在遊戲中展開，在遊戲中建立。

卡比爾說，整個世界

棲身在祂的遊戲中，

而遊戲者仍是未知者。

卡比爾之歌

III.84. jhī jhī jantar bājai

THE harp gives forth murmurous music; and the
    dance goes on without hands and feet.

It is played without fingers, it is heard without
    ears: for He is the ear, and He is the listener.

The gate is locked, but within there is fragrance:
    and there the meeting is seen of none.

The wise shall understand it.

083

豎琴奏出低沉的音樂；

無需手足的舞蹈在繼續。

豎琴彈奏，卻無需手指，

音樂聽見，卻無需耳朵：

因為祂就是耳朵，祂就是聽者。

門鎖上了，但屋裡充滿了芳香：

那裡的相會沒人看見。

智者自會明白其中的含義。

III.89. mor phakīrwā māṅgi jāy

THE Beggar goes a–begging, but I could not
  even catch sight of Him:
And what shall I beg of the Beggar?
He gives without my asking.
Kabir says: "I am His own: now let that befall
  which may befall!"

084

乞丐在乞討，但我甚至看不見祂：
而我應向乞丐乞討什麼？
祂施捨，無須我開口。
卡比爾說：「我就是祂自己的：
現在就讓要降臨的降臨！」

III.90. naihar se jiyarā phāṭ re

MY heart cries aloud for the house of my lover;
the open road and the shelter of a roof are
all one to her who has lost the city of her
husband.

My heart finds no joy in anything: my mind and
my body are distraught.

His palace has a million gates, but there is a vast
ocean between it and me:

How shall I cross it, O friend? for endless is the
outstretching of the path.

How wondrously this lyre is wrought! When its
strings are rightly strung, it maddens the
heart: but when the keys are broken and the
strings are loosened, none regard it more.

085

我的心在大聲哭泣，為了我戀人的房屋；

她已失去她夫君的城市，

對她來說，大街和庇護所都是一樣。

我的心找不到任何樂趣：

我的身體和頭腦都在發狂。

祂的宮殿有萬千扇門，但中間的海洋將我們阻隔：

哦，朋友，我要如何遠渡重洋？

這漫漫長路無窮無盡。

這七弦琴製作得多麼精緻！

它的琴弦一旦調準，它能讓心瘋狂：

但當琴鍵破碎，琴弦鬆脫，

沒有人會再多看它一眼。

I tell my parents with laughter that I must go to
my Lord in the morning;

They are angry, for they do not want me to go,
and they say: "She thinks she has gained such
dominion over her husband that she can
have whatsoever she wishes; and therefore
she is impatient to go to him."

Dear friend, lift my veil lightly now; for this is
the night of love.

Kabir says: "Listen to me! My heart is eager to
meet my lover: I lie sleepless upon my bed.
Remember me early in the morning!"

我大笑著告訴我的父母，

我一早就要上路，前往真主那裡；

他們惱怒萬分，因為他們不想讓我離開，

他們說：「她以為她已牢牢控制夫君，

她就能為所欲為；所以，

她迫不及待要去她夫君那裡。」

親愛的朋友，現在輕輕揭開我的面紗；

因為這是愛之夜。

卡比爾說：「請聽我說！

我的心渴望與我的戀人相見：

我躺在床上無法入眠。

請在清晨將我思念！」

III.96. jīv mahal meṉ Śiv pahunwā

SERVE your God, who has come into this
  temple of life!
Do not act the part of a madman, for the night is
  thickening fast.
He has awaited me for countless ages, for love of
  me He has lost His heart:
Yet I did not know the bliss that was so near to
  me, for my love was not yet awake.
But now, my Lover has made known to me the
  meaning of the note that struck my ear:
Now, my good fortune is come.
Kabir says: "Behold! how great is my good
  fortune! I have received the unending caress
  of my Beloved!"

086

服侍你的神吧，

祂已走進這座生命的神殿！

不要像瘋子一樣，因為很快就夜深了。

祂已等了我無數歲月，

為了對我的愛，祂已失去了祂的心：

而我從前卻不知道，至福離我如此之近，

因為我的愛還沒有醒來。

但現在，摯愛已讓我明白，

我耳中響起的音符之意；

現在，我的好運已經到來。

卡比爾說：「看哪！我是多麼幸運！

我已得到我的摯愛無盡的寵愛！」

I.71. gagan ghaṭā ghaharānī, sādho

CLOUDS thicken in the sky! O, listen to the
    deep voice of their roaring;
The rain comes from the east with its mono-
    tonous murmur.
Take care of the fences and boundaries of your
    fields, lest the rains overflow them;
Prepare the soil of deliverance, and let the
    creepers of love and renunciation be soaked
    in this shower.
It is the prudent farmer who will bring his
    harvest home; he shall fill both his vessels,
    and feed both the wise men and the saints.

087

天空的雲層越積越厚！

哦，請聽它們低沉的吼聲；

大雨由東而來，一路發出單調的低語。

查看你的籬笆和圍欄，以免雨水氾濫；

準備掘開堤壩，

讓愛和解脫的爬藤在大雨中浸潤。

只有謹慎的農夫才能將他的收穫帶回家；

他將堆滿他的穀倉，供養智者和聖人。

III.118. āj din ke main jāun balihārī

THIS day is dear to me above all other days, for today
the Beloved Lord is a guest in my house;

My chamber and my courtyard are beautiful with His
presence.

My longings sing His Name, and they become lost in
His great beauty:

I wash His feet, and I look upon HisFace; and I lay
before Him as an offering my body, my mind, and
all that I have.

What a day of gladness is that day in which my Beloved,
who is my treasure, comes to my house!

All evils fly from my heart when I see my Lord.

"My love has touched Him; my heart is longing for the
Name which is Truth."

Thus sings Kabir, the servant of all servants.

088

於我而言，今天要比任何一天都可愛，

因為在今天，摯愛的真主來我家作客；

祂的光臨，讓我家蓬蓽生輝。

我的渴望唱出了祂的真名，

同時全都沒入祂極度的美之中：

我為祂沐足，我端詳祂的容顏；

我躺倒在祂面前，將我的身心和所有作為獻禮。

今天，我多麼歡樂開懷，

今天，我的摯愛、我的珍寶光臨我家！

當我看見了真主，

我心中所有的邪惡都遠離了我。

卡比爾——所有僕人的僕人

這樣唱道：

「我的愛已觸摸到祂；

我的心渴望真理之名。」

卡比爾之歌

I.100. koī śuntā hai jñānī rāg gagan meṇ

Is there any wise man who will listen to that solemn
   music which arises in the sky?
For He, the Source of all music, makes all vessels full
   fraught, and rests in fullness Himself.
He who is in the body is ever athirst, for he pursues
   that which is in part:
But ever there wells forth deeper and deeper the
   sound "He is this——this is He"; fusing love and
   renunciation into one.
Kabir says: "O brother! that is the Primal Word."

089

有哪一位智者會聆聽空中升起的莊嚴音樂？

因為祂——一切音樂之源

將所有的容器充滿，並安棲在祂的充滿之中。

肉身之人永遠渴望，

因為他總是追求著其中的部分：

但總是從更深處冒出一個聲音：

「這就是祂，這就是祂」；

將愛和解脫融合為一。

卡比爾說：「哦，兄弟！

這是根本之言。」

I.108. maiṉ kā se būjhauṉ

To whom shall I go to learn about my Beloved?
Kabir says: "As you never may find the forest if
  you ignore the tree, so He may never be
  found in abstractions."

090

我要從誰那裡瞭解我的摯愛？
卡比爾說：「如果你忽略了樹木，
你就永遠找不到森林，
因此，在抽象的觀念中，
你永遠不會找到祂。」

卡比爾之歌

III.12. saṃskirit bhāshā paḍhi līnhā

I HAVE learned the Sanskrit language, so let all
    men call me wise:
But where is the use of this, when I am floating
    adrift, and parched with thirst, and burning
    with the heat of desire?
To no purpose do you bear on your head this
    load of pride and vanity.
Kabir says: "Lay it down in the dust and go forth
    to meet the Beloved. Address Him as your
    Lord."

091

我已學會梵文，好讓所有人來誇我聰明：
但當我隨波逐流，又熱又渴，
受著內心欲望的煎熬，這又有何用？
你頭頂著驕傲和浮華的重負卻無用處。
卡比爾說：「把它放入塵土，
去與摯愛相會。
稱祂為你的真主。」

III.110. carkhā calai surat virahin kā

THE woman who is parted from her lover spins
at the spinning wheel.
The city of the body arises in its beauty; and
within it the palace of the mind has been
built.
The wheel of love revolves in the sky, and the
seat is made of the jewels of knowledge:
What subtle threads the woman weaves, and
makes them fine with love and reverence!
Kabir says: "I am weaving the garland of day and
night. When my Lover comes and touches
me with His feet, I shall offer Him my
tears."

092

婦人在紡車前紡紗，
她已與她的戀人分離。
美麗的身體之城升起；
其中的思想宮殿已經建好。
愛之輪在天空旋轉，
座椅由知識的珍寶做成：
婦人紡織的紗線是如此精緻，
她懷著愛和敬重將它們織出完美！
卡比爾說：「我在紡織日夜的花環。
當我的摯愛到來，
祂會用祂的雙腳觸碰我，
我獻給祂的將是我的淚水。」

III.111. koṭīṉ bhānu candra tārāgaṇ

BENEATH the great umbrella of my King millions of suns and moons and stars are shining!

He is the Mind within my mind: He is the Eye within mine eye.

Ah, could my mind and eyes be one! Could my love but reach to my Lover! Could but the fiery heat of my heart be cooled!

Kabir says: "When you unite love with the Lover, then you have love's perfection."

093

在我的國王的巨傘之下，
千萬顆日月星辰在閃耀！
祂是我心中之心，祂是我眼中之眼。
啊，但願我的心和眼能夠合一！
但願我的愛能抵達摯愛那裡！
但願我火熱的心能得到冷卻！
卡比爾說：「當你將愛與摯愛合一，
你就會擁有愛的完美。」

I.92. avadhū begam deś hamārā

O SADHU! my land is a sorrowless land.

I cry aloud to all, to the king and the beggar, the
emperor and the fakir——

Whosoever seeks for shelter in the Highest, let
all come and settle in my land!

Let the weary come and lay his burdens here!

So live here, my brother, that you may cross with
ease to that other shore.

It is a land without earth or sky, without moon
or stars;

For only the radiance of Truth shines in my
Lord's Durbar.

Kabir says: "O beloved brother! naught is
essential save Truth."

094

哦，苦行僧！

我這裡是無憂之地。

我向所有人呼喊，

國王和乞丐，皇帝和托缽僧——

無論誰想在至高處尋求庇護，

就讓他來我這裡居住！

讓疲憊者前來，在這裡卸下他的重負！

就在這裡生活，我的兄弟，

你會輕易抵達彼岸。

這裡沒有天空大地，沒有皓月繁星；

在真主的客廳，只有真理的光芒閃耀。

卡比爾說：「哦，親愛的兄弟！

還有什麼比真理更重要？」

I.109. sāī<u>n</u> ke saṅgat sāsur āī

I CAME with my Lord to my Lord's home: but
   I lived not with Him and I tasted Him not,
   and my youth passed away like a dream.
On my wedding night my womenfriends sang
   in chorus, and I was anointed with the
   unguents of pleasure and pain:
But when the ceremony was over, I left my Lord
   and came away, and my kinsman tried to
   console me upon the road.
Kabir says: "I shall go to my Lord's house with
   my love at my side; then shall I sound the
   trumpet of triumph!"

095

和我的真主一起來到真主家中：
但我不曾和祂一起生活，也不曾瞭解祂，
我的青春已消逝如夢。
哦，在我的新婚之夜，
我的女伴們同聲歌唱，
我接受了塗油禮，塗以歡樂和痛苦的油膏；
但當婚禮結束，我離開了真主，
在路上，我的親人想安慰我。
卡比爾說：「我要帶著我的愛在身邊，
回到真主的家中；
接著，我要吹響勝利的號角！」

I.75. samajh dekh man mīt piyarwā

O FRIEND, dear heart of mine, think well! if
you love indeed, then why do you sleep?

If you have found Him, then give yourself utterly,
and take Him to you.

Why do you loose Him again and again?

If the deep sleep of rest has come to your eyes,
why waste your time making the bed and
arranging the pillows?

Kabir says: "I tell you the ways of love! Even
though the head itself must be given, why
should you weep over it?"

096

哦，我親愛的朋友，好好想想！

如果你真的墜入愛河，為何你還在沉睡？

如果你已找到了祂，

那就將你自己徹底奉獻，

把祂帶入你之內。

為何你一次又一次將祂放開？

如果你已睡眼朦朧，

為何還要浪費時間去鋪床疊被？

卡比爾說：「讓我來告訴你愛之道！

為何要為你的頭顱哭泣，

如果你必須將它獻出？」

II. 90. sāhab ham men, sāhab tum men

THE Lord is in me, the Lord is in you, as life
is in every seed. O servant! put false pride
away, and seek for Him within you.
A million suns are ablaze with light,
The sea of blue spreads in the sky,
The fever of life is stilled, and all stains are
washed away; when I sit in the midst of that
world.

Hark to the unstruck bells and drums! Take your
delight in love!
Rains pour down without water, and the rivers
are streams of light.
One Love it is that pervades the whole world,
few there are who know it fully:

097

真主就在我心中，真主就在你心中，
正如生命在每一顆種子之中。
哦，僕人！別再妄自尊大，
在你之內將祂尋找。
千萬顆太陽在閃耀，
蔚藍的大海與天相連，
當我端坐在世界的中央，
生命的狂熱變得寂靜，
所有的污穢被清洗乾淨。

聆聽這不敲自響的鐘鼓！在愛之中歡喜！
無水之雨傾盆而下，河裡流動著光芒。
合一之愛遍滿世界，但很少有人完全明白：

They are blind who hope to see it by the light
 of reason, that reason which is the cause of
 separation——
The House of Reason is very far away!

How blessed is Kabir, that amidst this great joy
 he sings within his own vessel.
It is the music of the meeting of soul with soul;
It is the music of the forgetting of sorrows;
It is the music that transcends all coming in and
 all going forth.

誰想用理智之光將它看清，誰就是瞎子，

理智是分離的原因——

理智之屋相距遙遠！

卡比爾是多麼有福，

他在自己內在，歌唱出極度的喜悅。

這是靈魂與靈魂相遇的音樂；

這是忘卻悲傷的音樂；

這是超越所有熙來攘往的音樂。

II.98. ṛitu phāgun niyaṛ ānī

THE month of March draws near: ah, who will
    unite me to my Lover?
How shall I find words for the beauty of my
    Beloved? For He is merged in all beauty.
His colour is in all the pictures of the world, and
    it bewitches the body and the mind.
Those who know this, know what is this
    unutterable play of the Spring.
Kabir says: "Listen to me, brother! there are not
    many who have found this out."

098

三月之唇已經靠近；

啊，誰會讓我和我的摯愛結合？

我要如何形容我的摯愛的美麗？

因為祂與所有的美麗相融。

祂的色彩在世上所有的圖畫中，

它迷住了身體和心靈。

知曉這一點的人，

就知曉這無法言說的春天的遊戲。

卡比爾說：「兄弟，請聽我說，

很少人明白這一點。」

II.111. Nārad, pyār so antar nāhī

OH Narad! I know that my Lover cannot be far:

When my Lover wakes, I wake; when He sleeps,
I sleep.

He is destroyed at the root who gives pain to my
Beloved.

Where they sing His praise, there I live;

When He moves, I walk before Him: my heart
yearns for my Beloved.

The infinite pilgrimage lies at His feet, a million
devotees are seated there.

Kabir says: "The Lover Himself reveals the glory
of true love."

099

哦，納拉德 [22]！

我知道我的摯愛並不遙遠：

當我的摯愛醒來，我就會醒來；

當祂入睡，我就會入睡。

誰要讓我的摯愛受苦，

他就會被徹底摧毀。

他們在哪裡歌唱祂的頌歌，我就在哪裡生活；

當祂動身，我就走在祂前面：

我的心渴望著我的摯愛。

無限的朝聖之路在祂腳下，

無數的崇拜者坐在那裡。

卡比爾說：「摯愛祂自己會顯現真愛的榮耀。」

II.122. kōī prem kī peṅg jhulāo re

HANG up the swing of love to-day!

Hang the body and the mind between the arms

    of the Beloved, in the ecstasy of love's joy:

Bring the tearful streams of the rainy clouds to

    your eyes, and cover your heart with the

    shadow of darkness:

Bring your face nearer to His ear, and speak of

    the deepest longings of your heart.

Kabir says: "Listen to me, brother! bring the

    vision of the Beloved in your heart."

100

今天就架起愛的鞦韆！

在愛的狂喜中，將身心都掛在摯愛的臂彎；

將烏雲的淚雨帶到你的眼裡，

用黑暗的陰影遮蓋你的心：

將你的臉貼近祂的耳朵，

訴說你心中最深的渴望。

卡比爾說：「兄弟，請聽我說！

將摯愛的形象帶進你的心中。」

注 釋

1. 此處的「我」專指神。——中譯者注，下同。

2. 天房（Kaaba）：麥加大清真寺內的一座方形石殿，內有神聖黑石，為穆斯林朝覲的中心。

3. 伽拉薩山（Kailash）：印度教認為它是世界的中心，濕婆神居住之地。

4. 拉維達斯（Raidas）：鞋匠，卡比爾的朋友和門徒。

5. 幻相（maya）：即「摩耶」，指物質世界。

6. 梵天（Brahma）：印度教三大主神之一，至高神。

7. 音流（the Word）：即夏白德（Shabd），又稱納姆（Naam），是靈魂與梵天溝通的方式。專注於音流的終極目標就是與梵天融為一體。

8. 天鵝：象徵靈魂。

9. 桑雅士（sanyasi）：古魯的門徒。

10. 黑天神（Krishna）：印度教中毗濕奴的第八個和主要的化身。

11. 毗濕奴（Vishnu）：印度教三大主神之一，世界的保護者和維持者。

12. 濕婆（Shiva）：印度教三大主神之一，世界的毀滅者和重建者。

13. 因陀羅（Indra）：印度教中的雷雨之神。

14. 朱木納河（Jumna）：在印度北部，與恆河匯合。

15. 唵（Om）：最主要和最神聖的一個音節，由梵語的三個音 (a)、(u) 和 (m) 構成。

16. 郭拉洽（Gorakhnath）：一個篤信濕婆神的瑜伽行者。

17. 貝拿勒斯（Benares）：印度北部聖城，現稱瓦拉納西。

18. 拉瑪南達（Rāmānanda）：卡比爾的上師。

19. 《往世書》（the Purāṇa）：印度史詩，由有關創世、神、萬物進化等的十八篇史詩組成。

20. 馬圖拉（Mathura）：印度北部城市。

21. 薩拉斯瓦蒂河（the Sarasvati）：印度傳說中的河流名。

22. 納拉德（Narad）：印度聖人和旅行家，毗濕奴的崇拜者。

InSpirit 25

卡比爾之歌 *SONGS OF KABIR*

100 首靈性詩選 [中英對照]

作　　者	卡比爾 Kabir
英　　譯	泰戈爾 Rabindranath Tagore
中　　譯	萬源一
責任編輯	席　芬
副總編輯	劉憶韶
總 編 輯	席　芬
社　　長	郭重興
發行人兼 出版總監	曾大福
出 版 者	自由之丘文創事業／遠足文化事業股份有限公司
發　　行	遠足文化事業股份有限公司
	231 新北市新店區民權路 108-2 號 9 樓
電　　話	02 2218 1417　傳真 02 8667 1065
劃撥帳號	19504465　戶名：遠足文化事業股份有限公司
封面設計	羅心梅
印　　製	前進彩藝有限公司
法律顧問	華洋法律事務所 蘇文生律師
定　　價	320 元
初版一刷	2018 年 11 月

ISBN 978-986-96958-2-4

Printed in Taiwan　ALL RIGHTS RESERVED

國家圖書館出版品預行編目 (CIP) 資料

卡比爾之歌：100 首靈性詩選 [中英對照] ／
卡比爾 (Kabir) 作；泰戈爾 (Rabindranath
Tagore) 英譯；萬源一 中譯 .-- 初版 .-- 新
北市：自由之丘文創，遠足文化，2018.11
　　面；　公分 . -- (InSpirit；25)
中英對照
譯自：Songs of Kabir
ISBN 978-986-96958-2-4(平裝)

868.951　　　　　　　　　107017504